Praise for Christian Baines

"Baines' brave new underworld is well devised, multi-layered, and dense with political and personal agendas—and it's frightening: so much so that I found myself looking over my shoulder more than once at night." FELICE PICANO, author of *Like People in History*

"Believable characters and rich settings pulled me into this world, and I didn't want to leave it. I was sorry to reach the end." GREG HERREN, author of the *Chanse MacLeod Mysteries* and the *Scotty Bradley Mysteries*

"A wickedly subversive wit." JEFFERY ROUND, author of *The Dan Sharp Mysteries*

"Baines has a gift for twisted psyches, playing the supernatural to expose the human evils at play, and a talent for turns of phrases that leave you shuddering even as you turn the page." 'NATHAN BURGOINE, author of *Light*

"Just fantastic! I just couldn't put it down." SARINA, *Love Bytes Reviews*

"5 stars! ...a devastatingly good read!" CAMILLE, *Joyfully Jay*

"Christian Baines is a writer with a bold, original vision, a vision not beholden to the limits of conventional genre tropes. This is a writer who knows his own voice, and a writer to watch." MICHAEL ROWE, author of *Enter, Night*

To Jamahl,
Hope you enjoy this
getting under your skin.

Christian B

BY CHRISTIAN BAINES

THE ARCADIA TRUST *series:*
The Beast Without
The Orchard of Flesh
Sins of the Son

Other books:
Puppet Boy
Skin

CHRISTIAN BAINES

SKIN

Christian Baines has written on travel, theatre, film, television, and various aspects of gay life, factual and fictional. Some of his stranger thoughts have spawned novels, including queer urban fantasy series *The Arcadia Trust*, the horror novella *Skin*, and *Puppet Boy*, which was a finalist for the 2016 Saints and Sinners Emerging Writer Award.

Born in Australia, he now travels the world whenever possible, living, writing, and shivering in Toronto, Canada on those odd occasions he can't find his passport.

SKIN

EDITOR: JERRY L. WHEELER
COVER DESIGN BY MELODY POND

Acknowledgements

Thank you to all who have stared into the gaping maw of Queer horror and speculative fiction and said "more please."

Thank you to the team at Bold Strokes Books for first unleashing Skin into the world, and especially to my editor, Jerry L Wheeler, for all of your support, encouragement, enthusiasm, and kindness on this project and others.

Special thanks to Canadian writing peeps Jeffrey Round, 'Nathan Burgoine, Stephen Graham King, Anita Dolman and James Moran among others for all your encouragement, practical advice, and for adopting me as one of your own.

A huge thank you to my beta readers, Avylinn for keeping me focused; Lynn Lorenz and Greg Herren, my NOLA experts for keeping me honest; and Dean, my favourite grumpy cat.

Thanks to the many friends, close family, and readers who've cheered me on, come to signings or launches, or just let me rave about whatever idea has got me excited in that moment.

I am deeply privileged to have you all.

SKIN

By Christian Baines

ANTOINE

He kissed the cold surface of the mirror, feeling it peel away the excess dark paint that announced his otherwise thin, unremarkable lips to the world. A simple ritual that would protect his boyfriend from wearing a thickly smeared Kryolan grin, just as it protected his own confidence. No doubt about it. Tonight, he was one highly kissable bitch.

He didn't say it aloud. The thought was enough to boost his ego as he smoothed the lapels of his favorite navy blazer and checked the seams of stockings that emerged perpendicular to the low, well-cut hem of his pants. Heels sensible enough to make him feel powerful, yet playful enough to suggest mischief housed his perfectly shaped size ten feet.

It had to be perfect. Almost a week had passed since he'd last seen Kyle. They'd never gone that long before, and Kyle had been cagey in his texts in the past few days. He'd decided not to read too much into it. Kyle wasn't the most emotional or demonstrative guy to begin with. It just meant that tonight, everything had to be on point.

The stockings were the only feminine indulgence beneath his pants-suit facade. No frilly silk prison for breasts that would never round out his flat, dark chest, its skin disappearing smoothly behind the shiny buttons of his red satin shirt. On a scene crammed with wannabe queens, baby

Ru-girls, and Masc4Mascs, the line he walked between male and female ensured he would always be his own man.

He turned to the image of Saint Grace that had adorned his wall since he was eight years old. The one that had survived regular threats of burning from his mother, who insisted that under her roof, even slaves to the rhythm would adhere to their designated bed time.

Saint Grace never smiled back at him, but that didn't matter. He smoothed his tightly buzzed hair, knowing he had her blessing.

Slay all those bitches, Mama. Slay. Them. All.

*   *   *

The click of his shoes seemed louder than normal, echoing off the fronts of long houses that lined the street. This corner of the Tremé, an uncharacteristic bubble of money near Esplanade and Rampart, wore the area's heritage in name only, kept afloat by cutesy couples, a lot of them queer, ageing gracefully into domesticity in their elegantly revived double shotguns and occasional camel-backs. He couldn't see himself ever growing old like that, nor Kyle ever wanting to live like that, not that he'd ever be able to afford it. "White trash," his folks would doubtless say before laying into worse slurs if Kyle ever rubbed them the wrong way, which he inevitably would. This left no doubt in his mind. His family only grudgingly turned a blind eye to his...particular interests. They sure as hell did *not* need to know he'd been dating some newly blown-in white hayseed he'd picked up in a Quarter bar.

He forced his shoulders back, ignoring the cool wind as it swept down Rampart. The area was deserted, while the faint lights of Bourbon Street's unending party glowed above the Quarter's rooftops. Where were they meeting again? Oz? No, Lafitte's. He quickly remembered. That preppy bartender at

Oz had gotten some bug up his ass about Kyle of late. Most likely because that bug was as close to his ass as Kyle would ever venture.

The silence broke just as he approached the far side of Rampart.

"Hey Princess! Love the look!"

Catcallers. Nothing unusual. Nor was the inevitable question of how to respond, if at all. Tonight, however, the very thought had taken too long.

"Where you goin'?" the voice continued. "I said, 'love the look.'"

"Thank you, kind sir!" he shot back. He adjusted his path, turning toward the streetlights and brightly lit facades of Esplanade, only to have one of the assholes step right out into his way. He discreetly scanned the streets for a cab, knowing too damn well and too damn late that he should have gotten one from home. But the walk into the Quarter was so short and the nights had been so nice out this past week, he hadn't given it a single thought. He knew better than to stroll down Rampart after dark, but since the creeps had positioned themselves right on the same corner he'd crossed hundreds of times before, he had no choice.

"What's the hurry?" the guy continued. "Slow down some, I want to ask you something."

"Sorry, I'm already late." He tried to keep an earnest, bouncy flirtatiousness in his voice as his heels clopped neatly on the pavement.

The three were in front of him before he could take another step.

"Jee-zus H Christ," muttered one of them. "What kind of beat-up, half-assed faggot queen are you?"

"Don't be an asshole," the first one scolded, shrugging off the insult with a broad grin that was anything but sincere. "He don't mean nothing. Say sorry to the lady."

"I ain't no lady," he replied without thinking, stiffening his back to emphasize the flatness of his chest.

"Well then," the first one continued. "Apologize to this...most unique individual."

The one with the nasty mouth looked him over with undisguised contempt. "I'm sorry," he spat out, drawling as if each syllable caused him physical pain.

He offered them a stiff, cold nod before trying to go around.

"Hey wait a sec. I said I want to ask you something. We need you to settle this."

I told you, I'm late.

Sorry. Excuse me.

Go fuck yourself, redneck.

All these thoughts rose on the tip of his tongue, but he bit them back. Better to let the asshole talk. Better to let him make a fool of his damn self rather than think he was being made fun of.

"Trannies..."

"I'm sorry, what?"

"Trannies. Like you."

"Wait, wait, wait. No. You are way off base there, mister. You need to ask somebody else."

"Well, what the fuck are you, then?"

"Awww, Jesus! You gotta be rude like that?" the first one sneered again at his burly wingman.

The other guy, thin, weedy, and the smallest of the three, grinned.

"One question," pressed the one in the middle. "Come on. Don't tell me you ain't got time for one little question."

He looked the leader up and down one more time, taking in his wiry frame. Colorful tattoos disappeared up the man's sleeve, ending in the tail of a snake, poking out of the guy's collar, licking at his neck. Ratty blond hair framed a face not so hard on the eyes, otherwise. In fact, the guy was kind of pretty, now he noticed, with a strong nose, delicate, well-cut jawline, and high cheekbones, spoiled only by a chipped lower tooth, plus a malformed one upstairs. Total white trash. But cute white trash. The same pedigree as Kyle.

No. Scratch that. Kyle was a gentleman. This jackass had just lucked out on genetics.

"Go ahead," he conceded. "Ask."

The punk widened his sarcastic grin, making a show of the bastard tooth. "So, if a trannie—which I know you ain't, so don't go gettin' all agitated—but if a trannie blows you, right? I don't mean, like, love making and shit, just straight up suckin'. And let's say you drop your load down his—"

"Her."

"What?"

"Her throat. Let's say you dump your jizz down *her* throat. I got you. Go on."

"Right. Sorry. Her throat. Exactly. *Her* goddamn throat. That wouldn't make you a faggot now, would it?"

Weedy guy was in a fit of wheezing laughter as Burly piped up.

"Bullshit! Of course it fuckin' would. If the guy's still got his johnson—"

"Girl, Lou. Girl." The leader was grinning like a fool, a sincere grin in all its nastiness.

He shook his head, heart beating way too fast for some bullshit 'teachable' moment. "I really gotta go."

"Oh, sure, sure. Didn't mean to hold you up. Hey, where you going? I'll walk you."

"No thanks, I'm fine," he replied, trying to step around.

"You never did answer his question," the big one said, stepping in his path.

"No, no, you did not."

He flinched as the leader put a hand on his shoulder.

5

"Woah! Ease up on the attitude, some. It's just a question. I'll ask again. If a trannie's giving you head and you—"

He threw himself between the leader and the thin, wiry looking one, barging his way through with his slim shoulders and catching Weedy off guard. He was soon clear of the trio, only to hear the thundering of their feet behind him. But even in heels, low and modest as his might be, he was faster, just as he always had been. He rounded a corner and powered down Barracks, veering off as he reached the Cabrini playground. He turned a sharp left, then another right, toward a bar he remembered. It was no sure thing. It wasn't a tourist place, and the owners seemed downright arbitrary about when they'd open and for whom. But it was his best chance. Besides, if he'd already managed to lose the creeps, what did it matter? Still, he wasn't about to turn his nose up at safe walls and extra time up his sleeve.

There it was. Up on his left. He silently prayed as his feet pounded the cracked pavement…don't be dark. Don't be dark. Don't be—

Far from it. The sudden eruption of cheers from the place would have been loud enough to blow out the windows, had they not been open already. Never in his life had he been so grateful for game night.

He slowed just enough to compose himself before ducking inside. Still, the door slammed a little too loud behind him as the cheers subsided. A half dozen guys decked out in the instantly recognizable Saints' black, white, and gold turned and stared at the unexpected fusion of power-suited corporate bitch and Quarter fabulousness that now stood panting in the midst of their sacred shrine to the pastimes of manly America. Another intercept by the despised Falcons diverted any slow-rising fury. He may have been black. He may have been queerer than a three-dollar bill, fully decked out in makeup and heels. But in a French Quarter bar on the first game night of the season, even the smallest-minded bigot would wrap all these things up in a big bear hug before they'd drink with a fucking Falcons fan.

He tried to find a spot near the bar, far from the prying eyes of any rubber-necking asshole at the window before taking out his phone. Two new texts from Kyle. And he was late.

Where u at? This guy in my face won't take a hint.

He couldn't resist a faint smile. He'd always told Kyle he was too good looking to sit around in bars hoping nobody would come bothering him. He swiped over to the second message.

Fuck, this guy! I'm heading to Phoenix. Meet me there?

This time he didn't smile. Phoenix? *Phoenix*??? Goddamn it! His gaze involuntarily landed on his black stockinged feet and heeled shoes. Oh sure. A bunch of straight Saints fans who'd been drinking since three in the afternoon was one thing, but the manly men of Phoenix? Would they even let him in? Did he have time to at least wash his make-up—No. No, goddamn it! They let women in, to the ground floor at least. They let drag queens in. And after the night he'd had, just let any asshole 'no fems' queen try to get up in his face.

Sure. On my way. Xx

He hit send and brought up… Damn it. Of course Uber was charging surge rates for game night. Fuck.

"Hey, buddy! Get you something?" the bartender called to him through the din.

He shook his head. The cabs would be just as nuts as Uber. Besides, if the fucks who'd disrespected him on Rampart hadn't found him by now, they'd probably moved on to stir shit with some other poor bastard. Maybe a big Saints fan who'd lay one or two of them out. He smiled at the thought, pocketing his phone. He hadn't hung out in the Marigny for a long while, but he knew it well enough. It couldn't have been more than a ten-minute walk.

He silently let himself out of the bar and strode back toward Esplanade. He tossed a glance up toward the corner of Rampart as he crossed the neutral ground. He flinched as a loud *WHODAT?* came at him from the window of a passing flatbed. No sign of his laugh-a-minute friends. He could cut along Burgundy… No, Dauphine was closer. The clop of his heels echoed off the surrounding houses once more. Everybody knew the Marigny had been gentrified to all hell, but damn! Every fourth, maybe third house had something going on. Renovating, landscaping, construction of a sacrificial altar, who the fuck knew what these hipsters did to their yards? He heard an outraged roar from one of the houses. Obviously, a taste for craft beer at pricey brunches and a fervent devotion to football were not mutually exclusive.

"Hey, Princess. You get lost?"

Startled, he whipped around to see the trio's leader behind him.

The man shoved him hard against the concrete fence of a vacant corner lot. He winced as his head hit a 'Keep Out' sign with a loud clatter. Once he'd regained his feet and his senses, he realized the wingmen were nowhere to be seen. It was just the cute, tatted up hick, staring him down with a smirk he didn't like one bit.

"What's your problem, man? Why you running? We scare you?"

"Look, I told you, I got—"

"Just answer my question. *Did we fucking do anything to scare you?*"

The words barely got through to him. Could he run again? What did this guy want? Goddamn it, why was it so dark? Why was nobody else out on the street?

"What do you want?"

"Well, Jesus! I *want* to have a reasonable conversation if that's not too much to ask."

"Look, mister, I do not want to have a conversation with you. You do not know me. You are not going to get—" He fell silent as he heard the flick of a knife at belly height.

"Yeah, that's right. That's better. Now, I'm not gonna have to get all nasty and use this, *am I?*"

"Look...look man, I ain't carrying much money, but you can have it."

"You keep your goddamn money. I said, why the fuck you—"

"No," he got out. "No, I don't think it does."

"You don't think what does what? Go on, Princess. Tell me what you don't think."

"I don't think it makes you a faggot if a trannie sucks you off. Now please, just—"

The guy's eyes went wide as he turned around full circle, palms out, waiting for the applause of an audience that still hadn't fucking deigned to turn up. "Oh! Well, thank you very much. I'm glad you chose to clarify that, though it still don't answer my current, most pressing question."

"Yes. Yes, I did!"

"...which is, '*Why the fuck you running?*' Or did you just forget I asked you that?"

He shivered, the ache in his stomach rising as the guy drew closer. Hunger. Fear. Arousal. Disgust. "What do you want?"

Rum was on the guy's breath as he pulled his lips back to reveal his flawed teeth. "Let's ah...step inside here for a minute." The guy nodded at the rusted gate to nowhere in the middle of the fence.

He watched as the creep, knife still open and shining in the moonlight, broke open the gate with ease and beckoned him inside.

Once they were both off the street, the man turned him once more. "Hey, ah…Sorry I got a bit carried away out there. I'm not gonna lie to you. The other guys? They wanted to mess you up some. Especially Lou. Man, he's got this thing about certain types of people."

"But you don't? Despite, you know, holding a goddamn knife on me?"

"Total contrary." The guy raised his hands, making a show of tucking the blade away and pocketing it. "And you're right, that was rude. I'm sorry. That was not worthy. Hell, I was just trying to get your attention. I'm just out for a little fun, same as everybody else. I don't care what business you got going on. You sure are pretty enough, if you don't mind me sayin' that."

"Whoa, whoa." He shook his head. "Listen, you got the wrong idea. I don't do that."

The man's hands were on his shoulders, shoving him to his knees before he could dodge or fight them.

"And why the fuck not, huh?" the guy demanded, yanking off his t-shirt and slapping a row of smooth, hardened abs.

In that moment, all he could do is stare at the piece of ripped trailer trash taunting him. The drum-tight shape of the body, the smell of it, the tattoos, the tilted hips as the man pulled down the lip of his jeans. He hated the sick feeling slowly invading his stomach. He hated the guy's handsome face and his stupid grin.

"Ain't nobody gonna know but us, Princess. You say it don't make me a faggot? That's good enough for me."

"I'm not—"

The man's hand stung his cheek. He choked, straining to keep his temper as the guy opened his jeans. He stared at the long appendage that rose from a mass of tight, blond curls, grinning death's head clumsily inked just above them. It mocked him, dared him to lick precum from the ugly, swollen organ before taking it wholly in his mouth.

It was stupid, vain hope to think this would be over quickly. Or that Kyle wouldn't taste him. Then Kyle would know and never want to touch him again.

"I....I can't!"

"Yes, you can, bitch," the man barked, grabbing the back of his head and forcing the hard head against his lips.

"Fuck off!" He closed his lips tight, until the hand stung his cheek again, releasing a faint gasp that might as well have been an invitation to the thug's hungry sex. He took it in smooth, fast strokes, hoping with each one that the man was close. That it would be over in seconds. Then he could spit it out like a bad, rancid dream.

A minute dragged into two, then three. Stroke, stroke, lick, lick. The bitter salt of the bastard's precum bubbled at the back of his tongue. Hurry up. Jesus, fuck, just hurry up already. Why did the prick want this if he wasn't gonna come? He pushed his tongue out farther, stroking the intruder's flesh right down to its musky hilt. The creep praised his efforts with an appreciative moan. His tongue, his secret weapon. He worked it along the entire length of the man's shaft, expertly edging down the foreskin, trying not to gag as the fresh sourness of the man's uncovered head scraped his throat. With his talented tongue, he returned the flimsy sheath to its former position. Then rolled it back again, arching the back of his tongue to scrape along the slit.

"Oh, man! Where the...oh fuck! What are you—Oh, Oh!"

The man had already pulled away before Antoine realized what he was doing. The creep's cock erupted not a half second later, sending sour, white rivulets over his face. He felt it drip from his lips as more landed on his eyes and cheeks, across his lips. Bleeding down his face, pearly white seed now stained with ruined makeup. A brown and white swirled mess came away in his hand as he tried to wipe it away. One eye was stuck shut and stung from the wayward load. The other was blinded only by rage.

If only he'd been stronger or faster or...fuck! How could he have been so stupid? The anger went through him as he slowly rose to his feet. Fuck it all. He was strong. He was fast. A fearsome electric charge went through him as he flicked away the mess from his hand. Prick. You fucking bastard asshole. I. Am. *Fierce*.

"How do you like that, Princess? Gotta say, you got some mighty fine ski—"

The thick wad of spit, makeup, and cum smacked across the thug's face with a wet plop.

The man stood there at first, staring at him with nothing to conceal his disbelief. He had no makeup to ruin. No mask to shatter, except the asshole's pride. All his dignity was now destroyed, leaving them equals.

He raised his arms up in front of his face as the man cursed him, jumping back as the first blow glanced off his arm. The second was less forgiving. Driven harder this time by the man's rage, it collided with a soft spot right below his eye, snapping across his nose with a pain that exploded through the side of his face, all the way to his jaw. He could no longer tell where the thug had hit him, now barely able to distinguish one punch from many.

He staggered, legs failing as a hard shove unbalanced him. The dust of the vacant lot swirled up into his nostrils and mouth, mingling with spit, snot, cum, and yes, of course, blood now. Had he really expected anything different? Why the hell had he not just swallowed his damn pride with a mouthful of makeup and bolted?

"You just gonna lay down there? On the ground, useless faggot bitch?"

He barely heard the thug's words. The steel toe of the man's boot hit his side before he could move an inch. He buried a scream in his filthy sleeve, trying to ignore the blood he'd already coughed into it.

"You want to fight me? Come on then, get up. Get the fuck up and fight me! Stupid cocksucker!"

Pain tore through him as he tried, as if his rib cage was splintering beneath his skin. With an effort that felt like one of his shoulder blades was tearing loose, he steadied himself on one elbow, as far from the ground as his aching limbs would allow, before focusing on his breaths. In, out, in, out, He tried to slow them down, each one like a knife through his gut. In, two, three, four, out, two, three...Slave to the Rhythm.

"I said, do you want to fight me?"

He had just enough time to wonder if one of the kicks had dislocated his shoulder before seeing the final, fatal blow come right at his head.

MARC

Marc's head felt like it had gone under the propeller of an outboard motor. His gut didn't feel much better, and the flesh below the decorative scarring on his chest ached a dull throb. He forced one eye open, still trying to shut out the mercifully dim light that surrounded him.

Where the fuck was he? Had he blacked out again? He couldn't remember drinking so much. Now, staring into the grinning jaws of a stuffed alligator's head perched atop a mannequin, decked out in a top hat, a skull clutched in its dark hand, he could smell the incense and pepper. A Voodoo shop. He'd gotten pissed out of his fucking mind and staggered his way into one of the Voodoo joints that clipped tourists who came looking for 'the local culture.' He squinted at the dark, musty portrait that stared down at him. Some crazy-ass faggot dressed in… Fuck. Panties? He looked away, rubbing the bridge of his nose and easing up onto his feet. He picked his shirt up off the floor and slipped it over his head, dismissing the passing realization that it wasn't his usual style. He couldn't even remember buying it. Or stealing it. Why he'd taken it off was anyone's guess.

"Yes, that's right, Officer," he heard a faint, cranky-ass voice croak outside. "Dumaine. No, I don't think he'll give

you any trouble. But he's locked himself in there, and I can't…
No, I'm not looking to press charges! I just want my
goddamn… I'm not shouting, Officer."

Shit! Where was he? What had he gone and done?

Marc padded as quietly as he could to the door. He put a
hand on the knob and opened it as slow as he could manage,
hoping no creak or latch would give him away. But the man
outside seemed far too engrossed in his phone conversation
to hear much else. Marc couldn't remember how he'd gotten
in there, but if he could creep quietly enough around this
corner…

"Goddamn it!" the man shouted, ending his call and
turning to look Marc full in the face.

The two of them stood in silence for a moment. Marc
guessed the man at fifty, maybe sixty, and though he clearly
moved about with the aid of a shiny black cane, the glint in
the old guy's eyes gave no hint of time having slowed or
confused him. He looked Marc over from top to bottom, very,
very closely.

Marc opened his mouth to say something. Apologize? Ask
for the bathroom? Fuck!

"I think it's high time you left, son," the man said at last,
leading him with a slow step to the main door and turning the
lock. It swung open to reveal a darkening sky, with heavy
storm clouds chasing any persistent traces of sunlight.

Marc nodded, trying to pass nervousness off as respect as
he again straightened his clothes and made for the door.

The old guy arched an eyebrow at him as he passed. "Hope
you found what you were looking for."

As the first drops of an evening downpour hit his face,
Marc picked up his stride and ran.

KYLE

Alien. That was the only word for it. As alien a place as Kyle had ever seen in his life, from the lurid colors of the drinks to the shirtless guys doing the pouring. Their hard stomachs, strong backs and powerful arms rippled under the dim lights as they effortlessly mixed the cocktails, strong hands moving faster than Kyle could follow. Four bodies too built to be real. All part of the fantasy the bar used to loosen a few more dollars from its guests.

Several small gangs of girls were each crowded around one in a two-dollar plastic tiara, fairy lights blinking on and off as they stared into the dim blue light of their cell phones. A cute, but cocky-looking blond guy with tattoos and a weird tooth kept smiling at him, not to mention the elephantine drag queen fresh off the stage and now sipping a bright pink cocktail at the end of the bar, in between jokes with one of the bartenders.

The sound system boomed with some hideous pop song that sounded much like the one before it, and the one before that, and the one the drag had synched to. He couldn't remember any of their titles, or the names of the singers for that matter. He'd made himself a promise to check out every gay bar in the Quarter at least once to get a good feel for the place. Maybe find his little piece of it. But he'd soon given up on trying to find a place that played his type of music. New Orleans might have been a haven for every kind of weirdo and freak, but he guessed a gay dive bar that played punk rock might have been a stretch, even for the famously eclectic tastes of the Crescent City.

He looked down at the rapidly approaching bottom of his beer glass, then scanned the gyrating crowd again. A skinny black guy stood out half a head's height above the throng, pushing his way through the crowd of twinks and tourists. At last, the stranger reached the bar, where Kyle could get a good view. The man looked around his age, give or take. Twenty, maybe twenty-one or twenty-two. But he might easily have been a few years older, especially with what he was wearing.

Kyle's eyes widened as he had a good long look at the stranger's deep purple blazer. Ass-hugging pants were stretched tight over his long, sinewy, athletic legs with decent-sized feet encased in a low pair of black heels. The guy was wearing a girl's belt, too. As the lights flashed over the stranger's hands, Kyle was sure his nails were painted the same shade of purple. Now that he noticed it, the blazer was also meant for a girl.

The stranger waved his long, bony hand to get the bartender's attention, shouting just loud enough for Kyle to hear over the din. He'd braced himself for a braying, high-pitched whine like the drag queens he'd seen on TV. Instead, he heard only a polite, "Another one please, Miles," in a clear, well-bred voice. The voice of someone way more refined and educated than he'd ever be. With a nervous swallow, Kyle realized it had given him an instant hard-on.

"Well? What are you drinking?"

Kyle struggled for breath, realizing the striking creature had just addressed him. His mind struggled to keep up, trying to match the voice he'd just heard to the drag and makeup the guy had on. Most of the queens he'd seen at least tried to sound like women when they dragged up. Not this one.

"You...you look real pretty," he got out at last.

"Well thanks, but that wasn't my question."

"Oh! Ah...just Bud."

"Oh, no. No, no, no, that cat piss is what I'd order if I hated you." The stranger turned his attention back to the muscular bartender he'd been talking to. "Miles, can we please get this boy a Heineken, *at least?*"

"Oh, I didn't mean to, ah... That is, I wasn't..."

"On its way, handsome guy. The least you can do is share in some conversation. You don't object to being seen with a pretty boy, do you?"

Kyle took several deep breaths, hoping the queen wouldn't notice. "Well, no, of course not. Thanks. You'd be...more of a pretty girl though, wouldn't you?"

The stranger stood deathly still, eyeballing him, a bright green cocktail in one hand, and a nowhere near as bright green bottle with the familiar label in the other. "Now why would you say that?"

He shrugged. "Other queens I met, they all call each other 'girl,' 'her,' 'she,' or whatever."

"My friend, I've been called a great many things. What I am *not*..." He set down the beer emphatically. "...is a drag queen."

"I...I'm sorry. I didn't mean to—"

"You didn't."

"But still—"

"Forgotten."

"I just—"

"It's fine."

"So," he began again, only now realizing the stranger's lips were also painted purple. Was there a non-insulting way to finish?

18

"So, why all this?"

Kyle nodded.

"Because I like how it feels to know I make this look good," he said, pushing back his shoulders within the blazer. "And because once in a while it's nice to hear some handsome stranger tell me I look pretty. Someone I just happen to spy across the bar whose name is…"

"Huh? Oh, I'm sorry. The name's Kyle."

"Antoine Lavolier. *Enchanté*," the man said, extending his bony hand with the palm down.

Kyle stared at it a moment before taking gentle hold. Then, feeling clumsy as a horse in football cleats, he pitched forward and kissed the back of Antoine's fingers.

Antoine grinned, taking another sip of his drink. "Was that as hard as it looked?"

"Pretty much." Kyle lifted the familiar green bottle he'd seen and ignored countless times in bars back home and took a long pull. Though he screwed his nose up at first, he had to admit it went down easy.

"Dare I ask, Kyle, what godforsaken town spat you up?"

He offered up a small shrug. "Not a town, exactly. More like about fifty miles out of Shreveport."

Antoine stared at him. "That's it? Outside of Shreve-port? That's all I'm getting?"

"Close enough."

"Well, all right then, Kyle from fifty miles out of Shreve-port."

They sat in silence and near perfect stillness for a moment, watching the crowd. A trio of two boys and a girl scowled at another girl in a twinkling plastic tiara as she pushed them aside on her way to the bar. In the darkness of the upstairs balcony, Kyle spied two guys exchanging a blowjob where they thought they couldn't be seen. He caught the blond guy scowling at him before the man turned his back and moved away.

"Hey," Kyle said at last. "I don't want to keep you from your friends."

"I'm here alone," Antoine replied. "Unless, *you'd* rather be alone."

"Oh, no. I didn't mean that."

"Ahah, that black cloud over your head's just a freak weather accident, huh?"

Kyle offered up a grim flick of a smile. "The music kind of sucks."

Antoine nearly choked on his cocktail with laughter. "What would you prefer?"

"I don't know. I guess the gays ain't much into metal and punk."

"Sure they are. Just not the gays who come here."

"So, what do you like? Beyoncé and stuff, I guess?"

Antoine fixed him with a glare framed exquisitely with the darkest eyeliner Kyle had ever seen. "Do I need to explain what was wrong with what you said just now?"

"All right, all right," he said, raising his hands in surrender. "You don't like Beyoncé. Noted."

"I like Beyoncé just fine. Not the point, white boy. It's called profiling."

"Okay, okay. I get it. Sorry."

"It's fine."

"So, who do you like better?"

The shoulders of the blazer rose and fell with another shrug. "I like all kinds, on the understanding that Saint Grace reigns above all."

"Saint Grace?"

"Grace Jones?"

Kyle stared at him blankly.

"Aaaaand we are done." Antoine picked up his cocktail and started back toward the dance floor.

"Hey, wait a second," Kyle said, taking gentle hold of the man's blazer sleeve, releasing it at his stern glare. "Don't be like that. Who's Grace Jones?"

"Ask your Momma, Shreveport."

This time, Kyle felt the anger flicker through his own face.

An apologetic look seeped into Antoine's expression. "Sore spot, huh? I'm sorry, I didn't mean to be a bitch."

"You weren't."

"Well, I'm sorry."

"It's fine."

"Forgotten?"

"Forgotten."

The two of them couldn't help the silly grins that spread over their faces.

"Wait here," Antoine said, crossing to the DJ booth, pressing a banknote into the DJ's hand and whispering something in his ear. The man flashed them a smile as Antoine returned to take hold of Kyle's hand, barely giving him enough time to replace his beer on the bar.

"Hey, what are you—"

"Come on, Shreveport. Class is in session."

Kyle swallowed as the last howls of some generic, autotuned pop starlet faded from the sound system, replaced by a gently rising flow of sultry synthesizers, bleeding together in a song Kyle was sure he'd heard, but couldn't quite place. "I...I don't dance."

"You don't have to dance. Just move. I got you."

Kyle looked around nervously as several of the younger dancers vacated the floor. Most stayed. A few whooped in excitement as the synths rose again, and a forceful, female voice surged to meet them. He slowly began to sway his hips, trying to follow Antoine's movements, which flowed with an effortless grace Kyle could only envy.

"It's not about me," the man whispered in his ear.

After several deep breaths, Kyle felt himself bobbing back and forth, swaying gently in time to the music. Its rhythm picked up some bounce, and his movements quickly followed, feeling more and more natural as the lights flashed around him. He caught a glimpse of Antoine's broad grin as the man took gentle hold of Kyle's hand and leaned back.

"Yaaaaaaaassss!" Antoine bellowed, coming back up to full height, his smile brighter than ever. "Ladies and gentlemen, *le garçon de Shreveport* has arrived!"

"Geeze, will you pipe down?" Kyle muttered.

"You shouldn't be ashamed of having a good time."

"I'm not! I just… Jesus! Do guys actually say that? All that 'yaaaaaassss' stuff?"

Antoine burst out laughing, putting his hands on Kyle's shoulders and pulling him closer. "Only when there's something worth celebrating."

Kyle moved uncomfortably under Antoine's hands, only now noticing the stares. Dozens and dozens of eyes on the pair of them. The disheveled, unshaven white guy in the faded check shirt, jeans, and white t-shirt, next to Antoine, tall, dark, and flawless in his high fashion girly blazer, skin-tight trousers and perfect makeup. He slowed his dancing, trying to concentrate on the rhythm.

"Do you want to sit down?" Antoine asked.

He nodded immediately.

They returned to their seats at the bar, where Antoine ordered them two more drinks before Kyle could stop him.

"You did pretty good out there," he said in Kyle's ear. "Don't move. I'll be right back."

Before Kyle could say so much as 'thanks,' the guy was gone. Kyle took out his wallet as the bartender Antoine had called Miles brought their drinks.

"It's taken care of," the bartender said, setting them down and moving on to serve a fit, balding guy around the corner of the bar.

Kyle folded his bills away, save a couple of bucks tip in case Antoine had forgotten. Damn it, he could pay his own way. Maybe not far. He'd need a job soon enough. But he hadn't come to New Orleans for anyone's charity.

"You made yourselves quite a show out there."

He turned to see the speaker, the cute-ish blond dude who'd caught his eye before. The man leaned on the bar, one side of his mouth raised in a half smile that unsettled Kyle in a way that made him want to take a swing at the guy.

"Did you hear me? I said—"

"I heard you," Kyle said, taking a pull of his beer.

The blond guy grinned at him, his perfect upper set of white teeth marred by a single malformed canine. "You like her? Her highness?"

"Huh?"

The man nodded in the direction Antoine had gone.

"*He's* fine," Kyle muttered.

"Whoa, okay there, stud. No judgment. Just thought you'd go with someone more your type is all."

Kyle's frown deepened as he noticed the guy had drawn closer, their faces now just inches apart. "What do you think is my type?"

"You know. A man's man."

"You mean someone like you?"

"Now, I didn't say that, necessarily," the stranger leaned in to whisper in Kyle's ear. "Though you did look pretty funny out there with that nigger."

Kyle forced him away with a hard shove, only to cop a furious, silent snarl from the stranger and a cautionary look from the bartender. Out the corner of his eye, he saw Antoine cutting back through the crowd.

"Everything all right?" Antoine asked.

Without waiting, Kyle pulled Antoine closer and kissed him hard on the lips. Antoine quickly returned it with just as much vigor. Kyle tasted the sweet juice of the cocktails he'd been drinking, and the sweet, soft flesh of his tongue as it explored his own.

"Whatever, faggots." The blond stranger eased himself off the bar and let them be.

Kyle gently broke from the kiss, trying to ignore the thick smear of makeup he could feel across his mouth. "Go to hell," he muttered after the asshole.

Antoine took a napkin off the bar and dabbed his own smeared mouth. "Just so we're clear," he began, "I'm going to assume you had a very good reason for doing that involving the douche you just chased off, but in the future? I don't much care for being kissed by some boy I just met who's out to prove a point."

"I'm sorry. That guy just—" Kyle reached out, gently touching Antoine's sleeve. "How would you rather I kissed you?"

The gleam of a smile returned to the man's dark eyes. "How about I show you?"

MARC

"Five dollars."

Marc swallowed, tossing a glance at the guys up on the bar as they gyrated and bent down to flirt with patrons eager to tuck tips into their jocks. "Actually, I'm just here to ask about a job."

"Yeah?" the guy answered, his expression unchanged, giving Marc nothing. "Friday night, you come in here, you get and you pay for the same show as everybody else. You want to work? Talk to Dan behind the bar."

Marc silently cursed, fishing five bucks he really couldn't part with out of his pocket and passing it over.

The guy finally smiled, stamping his hand with the lurid purple logo. "Don't worry, handsome. Guy like you'll earn it back in no time."

He shuffled inside, trying to ignore the hungry gazes of the guys nursing drinks by the wall, not yet settled on a firm focus for their lust. Marc waited for a break in between the dancers on the bar, watching one tall guy duck to avoid a low wooden beam before going back to his movements and tossing a cocky smile at a grey-haired customer to his right. Shit. Was that what this was gonna be? He felt a sudden strange and compelling urge to punch the bartender at the Pub who'd tipped him off.

"Rafael to the bar, please. Rafael, you're up next."

Marc watched one of the dancers hop nimbly down from the bar and scan the room until he found a patron whose gaze was fixed on him. The boy smiled in the guy's direction before disappearing behind a red curtain next to the pool table. Swallowing his nerves and pride, Marc took his chance to approach the bar. "Umm… Excuse me?"

"What can I get you?" the guy asked through several folds of reddened flesh carpeted in grey stubble.

"Actually, I'm uh, here about the job." Looking up just in time to see the built Latin guy coming out from behind the red curtain, he suddenly felt about ninety pounds underweight. And fat. Somehow both underweight and fat at the same time. And white. Far, far too white.

"Only jobs I've got are for dancers."

Marc fought every impulse to steal another look at the Latin guy, who'd fixed on entertaining a couple of suited guys at the bar beside him. "I…I can dance, I guess."

Without looking at him, the bartender raised his eyebrows. "That sounds like confidence. Stick around 'til it quiets down some, then show us what you got."

He nodded, averting his gaze from the perfectly bronzed sex god that crossed his path on the bar and taking up a relatively safe spot along the wall near the pool table. One of the dancers leaned across it to line up a shot, making a show of wiggling a perfectly rounded butt barely contained by blue briefs, all for the pleasure of a tall, older gentleman who watched with an unabashed smile.

At least if Marc was out of his depth, he could play pool. Maybe.

His gaze fell on the red curtain behind the table, with a hastily painted 'Employees Only' sign at its top. Employees?

Right. He had to remember that. This was just a job. It wasn't as if he knew anyone else in New Orleans or had any other leads. He'd take what he could.

"You know, it don't magically pull back just because you keep starin' at it," a sly voice chided him.

He faced the stranger, whose pale white skin stretched over a sinewy body marked up with a number of intricate tattoos. A bloody looking skull at the base of his stomach. A snake that coiled around one of his arms before finally biting into his wrist, and some kind of leopard-looking cat down the other. The guy was smiling at him, lips just far apart enough for Marc to make out his teeth. He couldn't hide the weirdly shaped one up top. Still, the guy was kind of hot. Handsome, too, thanks to the sharp lines of his jaw and cheekbones, all topped off with an unkempt mess of dirty blond hair on his head. Two piercing blue eyes ran Marc over from head to toe, then back again.

He tilted his hips to cover the uncomfortable stirring in his jeans. "Wasn't staring. Just curious."

The guy's grin pulled back to show his teeth in all their imperfect glory. "Everybody's curious their first time. Second time? Well...that's more than curiosity."

Marc nodded, pretending to understand. "You dance here?"

"What do you think?" The guy pushed back his shoulders to make a show of his body, clad only in a pair of tight black boxer briefs and sneakers.

Marc shuffled his feet. "You like it?"

"It's good enough. Get to have some fun, make some folks happy. Send 'em home with hard-ons." He laughed in a way that almost made Marc feel foolish, but the smile that followed immediately softened it. "Really your first time here, huh?"

Nod.

"So, what? Ain't you drinking?"

"Kind of kind of tight for cash right now. Sorry."

"Awww," the guy said, flashing a smile at an older couple of guys who were eyeing them before turning back to Marc. "Just as well I'd give you a dance for free then, huh?"

"You'd... Wait, what?"

The guy flashed him one last smile before ditching him for the silver daddies.

Marc swallowed. Now he felt like a damn fool, just standing there while a half dozen guys his age in jocks, shorts, briefs, or less worked the room, putting away the dollars—and tongues—of guys twice, maybe three times their age. Okay, maybe they weren't like models or porn stars or shit, but most had tighter abs or bigger muscles than him.

The guy who'd come up to him kissed each of the old guys on the cheek as one tucked a bill into his boxer briefs. The Latin guy hopped down with a jock full of bills, only to be replaced by some white dude even more pumped. A skinny guy grinned as one of the three women in the place slid a bill all the way down his chest, tucking it into the front of his waistband. So, this was what it was about. Even if they weren't God's fucking gift, these guys sure strutted around like they were.

This was dumb. He'd been an idiot. Spectacularly fucking dumb.

"Hey! Where you goin'?"

He turned to look at the blond guy, who'd returned just in time to head off his hasty retreat. "I don't think this is really my thing," he explained sheepishly. "Think I made a mistake."

"Comin' in here without cash? Yeah, you did. Here." The guy held out a glass of what looked like Coke. "You need to loosen up some."

"Umm... I don't think—"

"What? It's not roofied, you paranoid fuck." He grinned again in a way that made it impossible for Marc to feel offended. "It's a rum and coke. You look like you could use it."

Marc took the drink with a faint smile. "You talk to all the customers like that?"

"Only the ones I like enough to buy a drink." He put out a hand. "The name's Ash."

"Marc." He returned the handshake before lifting the drink to his lips. The bartender had been stingy on the pour, but in that moment, already on the verge of making a damn fool of himself, he didn't mind at all.

"So if you ain't here to drink, and you ain't here to tip, what brings you into this place, Marc?"

He gulped down a big sip of his drink. "Someone told me they were hiring dancers."

"Shit. Another one, huh?"

Marc winced, hoping Ash hadn't seen it.

"Dan's always hiring dancers. Guys come in here, they do a shift or two, thinkin' they're gonna make big money. Then when they don't, you never see 'em again. No great loss."

"You make okay money, though?"

"Nosy, ain't ya?" the guy said through his smile. "Yeah, I do all right. Expectations, man. It ain't a whole lot, but it's easy money. Dan seen you dance yet?"

"I…I ain't dancin' with that on the bar." He nodded at the white muscle guy who was kneeling down accepting a bill from a guy who then patted his ass.

"Who? Alex? Don't mind him. I'll tell you somethin' about this place. If you ain't got the body, use your face. If you ain't got the face, work your body. If you got both, dude, get the fuck out of here and do porn, or get in with one of the agencies."

"Agencies?"

"Yeah, you know. The big guns. They send dancers around to Atlanta, Dallas, Houston…like, to all the gay pride parades and shit. But you basically gotta be porn material to dance with them. Think Alex, but prettier. Alex with your face, maybe."

Marc laughed, almost choking on his drink. "You're full of shit."

"Dead serious, man. You see 'em at Decadence every year. Check 'em out if you don't believe me. You go to Decadence? Bet a guy like you'd do all right there."

He shook his head, letting the compliment pass him over. "Kind of new in town."

"I don't much like it myself. Too many faggots. Hey, no offence. When I say 'faggots,' I mean the real queens, not like… Hey, you ain't—"

"Now who's bein' nosy?"

Ash smiled again. "Okay, stud. I guess I deserved that. I dug my hole. Anyway, I don't care who or what you do. Neither does Dan. If you can fake it, you can dance. I'm not sayin' ignore the chicks. They got money as good as anyone else. Just don't let it look like you're givin' 'em special treatment or more attention than the guys. Dan fuckin' hates that. Turns off the regulars."

"Thanks for the tip."

"Where you stayin'?"

He stopped, feeling his mouth go dry as the words hit home. "I…umm…"

"Is this a hard question? Or just none of my business?"

"Well, it's kind of a guest house, I guess."

"Aww, shit. In the Quarter? Man, no wonder you ain't got money left. Hell, I got room at my place. You can—"

"You don't have to do that."

"Yeaaaaah, well, actually I kind of do. My roomie just up and took off. I mean, just fucked right *off*, the asshole. I guess I don't *have* to stay. I'm not on the lease or nothin'. My buddy set me up, but he wants cash. It'd just be easier if somebody took over. Keep it nice and quiet. You get me?"

Marc nodded. The guest house may have been a bug-ridden old hell hole with lousy air conditioning, but it had still managed to bleed him almost dry. For Ash to suddenly come out with an offer like that seemed almost too good to be true. But damn! Could he afford to say no? "How much?"

"Cheap enough between two guys. A hell of a lot less than you're payin', I promise you that."

He couldn't help but grin, drawing more of his drink. "I'll think about it."

"Kellan, to the bar please," the voice boomed over the sound system. "Kellan, you're up."

"Hey, that's me," Ash said, backing off toward the stairs that led up to the bar. "You think about it. And if Dan likes your dancin', you owe me a drink."

Marc watched Ash/Kellan nimbly hop up on the bar and shake his ass for the obvious pleasure of several onlookers. Damn it. He *was* thinking about it. He wasn't carrying that much extra weight. Hell, barely enough to see in this light. As for the scarring on his chest, well, most of the guys in here had tats. He had scars. Some guys had to find that sexy. His own unique markings.

Ash flashed him another smile as he stepped over a customer's cocktail with catlike agility. Marc felt the stir in his jeans once more. Ash wasn't just being friendly. There was real sex in that smile. He felt weirdly connected to the guy. Fated, even. If Marc had had the money, he would have strutted right over there and stuck twenty in the guy's shorts right now.

Yeah. He could do this. He had to do this.

KYLE

"You're telling me now you've never been to an art gallery? For real? Like, at all? Actually, why am I surprised?"

"Hey, they ain't exactly dropping fine paintings off the back of trucks back home, all right?"

Kyle couldn't see Antoine's broad smile as they lay on the grass, staring up at the tips of the palms that towered over the sculpture garden, along with the edges of various iron and tin sculptures that stretched into the sky. But he heard the quiet laughter soon enough.

"What?"

"You've got a sharp tongue there, Shreveport."

Kyle was about to defend himself when he felt the soft touch of Antoine's fingers on his jaw, gently tilting their faces toward each other so the man could kiss his forehead.

"A sharp tongue and a quick wit. I wouldn't have picked it, but I like it."

Kyle smirked, taking in the height of the massive gallery before returning his attention to the twisted, skeletal metal.

"You like that?" Antoine asked.

He squinted, holding up his hand to block the brutal sun. The heat that had felt so good on their naked chests a half hour ago, now seemed oppressive in the crushing humidity.

Kyle could feel cool trickles of sweat run from his chest and down his flanks, into the grass under his back. Not that it was an unwelcome sensation. Nor was the sweet smell of Antoine's skin, where rivulets of sweat ran away down the smooth, dark surface with each of the much thinner man's breaths.

"What's it supposed to be?"

"You tell me."

He concentrated harder on the weird spire that curved like a long, exaggerated spinal column from the shoulders of the main sculpture, towering above it in a smooth arc, like the monster's tail in *Alien*. Except, now that he looked closely, each vertebra was another figure, perched on the shoulders, covering the eyes of the larger one beneath it. It went all the way up from the shoulders of the poor son of a bitch standing at the bottom, blinded to the parade of goblin-looking fiends above his head. The tiniest one sat at the top, a mere dark spot in the air just above their heads as the sculpture curled over.

"Yeah," he admitted. "It's a pretty cool place."

"Not exactly the Louvre, but it's ours." Antoine eased himself up onto one elbow and rested there, stroking Kyle's arm. "You want to go inside?"

Kyle shrugged. Getting out of the heat did sound good, but he also just wanted to lay there looking at Antoine. Today, the guy had shown up without makeup. No girlie pants or shoes. Just shorts, a tank top, and comfy slip-ons, almost the same as him. Was something wrong? Had Antoine thought he was making Kyle uncomfortable? Shit. He didn't want to be responsible for that.

"No, I'm good," he answered. "Maybe another day. Not too hot out for you, is it?"

Antoine let out a warm laugh. "Like I told you. Born and raised. If I'm not used to it by now—"

"I just thought, you know, since you're not wearing your other stuff."

Antoine's smile dimmed, now seeming shy as he avoided Kyle's eye. "I…I didn't want you to feel uncomfortable."

"Uncomfortable?" Shit. Shit, shit, shit. He'd bit back the urge to say 'girly,' though he knew he'd done a lousy job of hiding it.

"I was worried you'd be ashamed to be seen with me."

Kyle gently took Antoine's chin in his hands, pulled it closer, and kissed him deeply. "Never," he said after the kiss broke. "I would *never* be ashamed of that. You can wear whatever you want when you're with me. If folks don't like it, fuck 'em!"

Antoine's smile returned, though he hid it behind tightly closed lips. He finally lost the battle to hold back tears, choking on them with a laugh. "Well, damn, Shreveport. You're about the sweetest idiot I ever met."

Kyle almost laughed before… "Huh?"

"I'm joking, you dope. You think I'd dress down for you, or for anybody else? I ain't wearing stockings or a blazer on a day like today. Wait til two, three o'clock, and that shit's hot and sticky as hell."

Kyle looked away just in time to see the bored looking guard approaching them.

Antoine caught hold of his hand and squeezed. "And then you have to go and get all sweet like that."

They kissed again.

"Off the grass in the garden please, fellas," the guard chided them.

"Sorry!" Antoine called, scrambling to his feet and helping Kyle up.

Kyle caught himself starting at the guard, just for a moment. The man gave them a slight nod, adjusting his overstretched belt before continuing on his rounds.

"Your type?" Antoine asked.

"Hell, no! I just thought… When we kissed, he seemed so cool about it."

"Uhuh. You're in New Orleans now. This ain't Louisiana, and it is most definitely not 'the South.' You ain't gonna shock nobody here, provided you ain't stupid. At least not by making out with a matching set of genitals."

Kyle winced before he could stop himself. He should have been used to Antoine's honesty by now. But that blunt way he had of just putting himself out there, and the way he talked about sex would still take some getting used to.

"Sorry." Antoine grinned as a bike passed them on the path heading back toward the Canal streetcar. "I forgot those virgin ears of yours."

"Oh, fuck that!" Kyle replied with a grin of his own. "You know I'm just not used to talking like that. Reckon my daddy would have belted me real good if I did."

"And you think what? That I was born and raised by some sex-positive, moon-worshipping flower people?" Antoine laughed again. "Man, I didn't even come 'til I was fifteen."

"Get out!"

"No! I swear to god. They sat me down when I was maybe twelve, thirteen I guess, and it had to be the most painful twenty minutes of my father's life. He's all, like, trying to talk about things without actually *talking* about anything, and he's saying things like 'you know what feels good,' and I don't know what the hell he's talking about. I just heard the word 'vagina' and I checked out, you know?"

Kyle cracked up laughing.

"I swear to god. I barely figured out he was talking about touching myself. I didn't even know stuff was supposed to come out. Hell, first time it happened, I thought I'd broken it."

Kyle's knees almost gave out as he doubled over, clutching his stomach and trying to catch his breath. "You...you thought..." he wheezed between howls. "*You?*"

"Hey, like I said, this was not the most sex-positive household. All they gave us at school was like, 'abstain, abstain, abstain, marriage, marriage, marriage'—"

"What about porn and stuff?"

"Oh, *after* that first time, sure. I was all over that. But up 'til then? No. I wasn't gonna risk getting my ass whooped."

"And when was the first time you...you know. With a real guy?"

"College."

"Freshman virgin, huh?"

Antoine's teeth showed brilliantly across his dark face. "And sophomore virgin, and—"

"Okay," Kyle interrupted through more laughter. "Your first time, Lavolier. *When?*"

Antoine paused, a flush of embarrassment crossing his face for the first time Kyle could recall. "College senior year."

"*What?*"

"Look, you gotta understand something, Shreveport. When a black family's got serious money in this town, they protect it. They protect the name, especially if they're Creole, because that's not just color. It's heritage. I mean, it's not like it's my momma and daddy's money. It was my granddaddy's restaurant, and he died when we were kids. We've just been living off it ever since. My daddy got into city hall based on *that name*. It took some favors through church and people like that to get him there, too. That requires a certain level of 'good standing,' as they call it. Ain't no way I was gonna rock that. I wasn't exactly on scholarship, you know? Anyway, my last year, I finally, *finally*, started going to some of the gay stuff. Mixers...nothing political. Because once your face is out there on record, joining in with that stuff, you are fair game. You

36

can't just say 'oh, that was somebody else.' Anyway, this one time, this guy finally convinced me to go to one of these parties in drag."

"Right. And this was the guy—"

"This was *not* the guy. And I can't say drag did a whole lot for me. But then, people knew it was me. They didn't care. I was just Antoine. Antoine in a wig. A costume. They laughed. I laughed. We danced. We drank. It felt…so fucking good. Totally liberating. That was when I realized I didn't need the costume. I could just wear a few bits and pieces I liked because I liked them. The nails. The shoes. Whatever I was in the mood for, you know?"

"Okay, and this leads to your first time how?"

Antoine laughed. "Damn! You are not letting me have *any* secrets, are you?"

"No, no I'm not," Kyle laughed. "Not now you brought it up."

"All right, all right. Look, there's not that much to tell. Tall, geeky white boy from Texas somewhere. He was drunk. I was drunk. This was not some great romance of our time. But he was sweet and a damn good kisser, as I remember. More than that, he made me feel sexy. Like, *actually* sexual. Even under all the shit I was wearing. I know…this is only two years ago, and it sounds so stupid. But it was the first time I'd felt like that."

"So," Kyle said, his jaw almost hurting from the smile now fixed on his face. "You never went back? I mean, to being the way you were, all scared of sex and stuff?"

"I never did, and I never will. I mean, my parents know. My mom always *knew*. But we don't talk about it. It's just, 'oh, he's different,' or 'he's artistic, that boy.' My grandma calls me a 'Quarter character' like they used to back in the day and leaves it at that. It's not great, but what choice have I got? It's not like they're up in my face about it. If I want to go out, I can. So long as I don't wind up in the newspaper kissing some guy or nothing, it's no big deal."

They walked on in silence for a bit, Kyle stealing occasional glances at Antoine. It seemed so weird. Of course the guy's parents knew. How could they not? But then, if they were rich Catholic types, how could they not freak? Or would that have been worse? Easier to risk somebody asking questions about their 'artistic' son than suffer the scandal of throwing him out. Or the risk of leaving him with nothing to lose, happy to sell his story on the back of their precious name. It made sense, but it was still the rule of a world completely alien to Kyle.

"Well, Shreveport, I'm waiting."

"Waiting for what?"

"Bitch, you don't get to drink my tea without pouring some of your own. Now, spill!"

"Huh? What are you talking—"

"*Who was he?* How old were you? Do your momma and daddy know? I'm guessing there's a big fat 'no' on the end of that last question."

Kyle mopped the sweat from his forehead, cringing in the sunlight as he wiped the back of his hand on his shorts. "You really want me to talk about that?"

"Well I don't need you to open up, all childhood trauma and Dr. Phil on me, but yeah. I want to know something about you. Like who was the first guy you kissed?"

"First guy I...? Shit, I didn't *kiss* a guy for a long time."

"Meaning what? What did you do? You mean to say you started even later than me?"

"No, I started years ago. Just, you know, stuff. I blew a couple of guys."

"Uhuh. Just how many years ago are we talking?"

"I dunno. I was...I guess thirteen."

"*Thirteen?*"

"On my uncle's farm. He'd always hire a couple of guys to help him out over the summer. Gets hotter than hell up there, so…fit guys, no shirts or nothing. Hell, I didn't know what I was doing. This one time, one of 'em was just looking at me kind of funny, and he's like… man. Built solid, you know? He's wearin' these ugly-ass sweat pants. Nothin' underneath 'em, and it's just… Next thing I know, there I go. On my knees and that was it."

"You were hooked." Antoine grinned. "So, did this guy come back?"

"Hell, it wasn't just him. Maybe he told his buddy or somethin', but next thing I know, he wants a piece of the action, too. Then the next season, new guys, same shit. After a while, I just learned when to catch 'em on break. Sometimes they'd be jerkin' off, thinkin' nobody was around. Guess that must have happened a lot. Then I'd be there, so why not?"

"Uh, because you were *thirteen*? That's why not."

"You think these guys cared about that? Not 'til we got caught, anyway."

"Okay. I wondered when this was coming. Your uncle called the cops?"

Kyle winced at the memory. "It don't exactly work that way up there. Poor guy couldn't have been older than you and me are now, and he weren't exactly built like some of the other guys neither. My uncle beat on him so bad he put him in the hospital. Shit, it wasn't like he could say nothin'. *Then* they would have brought in the cops. I thought for sure, though, my daddy was gonna give me the same. But he never said nothing. My uncle never said nothing. Things were just…different."

"Different, how?"

"Like, everything became 'fucking faggots' this, and 'cocksucker' that. My dad and my uncle, they were never exactly open-minded people. But after that happened, I started hearing them talk like that, very specifically. I knew what it meant. They didn't have to say anything *to* me."

Antoine's smile spread into a wide grin again. "Until you ran away to become *un personnage du Quartier!*"

He barely raised a smile in response.

"Sorry. Didn't mean to touch a sore spot." Antoine nodded at a small drinks cart set up on the corner of the park just ahead. "You thirsty? I'm dying over here."

"Uh, yeah," Kyle admitted, grateful for the distraction and change of subject. "*But I'll get...* Goddamn it!" Antoine had run off before he could finish. He grabbed the flimsy cotton of his tank and fanned himself until Antoine returned with two cold drinks in hand. He wasn't a big fan of Mountain Dew, but he sure as hell wasn't feeling picky either. He fished three dollars out of his wallet. "Here."

"Put it away," Antoine answered, thrusting the damp drink into his other hand.

"No, I mean it. Let me get my own, at least."

"You need to get a job first, handsome."

Kyle put the money away in his pocket. Antoine didn't need to know he had an interview already, if he could call it that. Not unless he got the job. But then, if he did, how the hell was he going to explain that his first job in New Orleans was dancing as a goddamn stripper? He guessed there was no shame in it. The bartender who'd tipped him off about the place said he'd danced there a few years back. Said it with an almost nostalgic gleam in his eye. From what little Kyle had seen and heard, New Orleans seemed to have its own magic code about stuff like that, and it sure as hell beat wearing his feet raw running up and down covered in sweat and scraps in some kitchen for minimum wage. *If* he got minimum wage. But he couldn't quite see Antoine going for it. Not if they were... Fuck, were they boyfriends? Kyle wasn't even sure he knew what that meant.

40

"What you staring at over there?"

Kyle hadn't been staring at anything. He didn't notice the long body of water that stretched between them and the nearest houses until Antoine spoke. He grabbed the opportunity to again change the subject. "What's that lake over there?"

"Over there? That's Bayou St John. Lot of history in that neighborhood. Supposed to be where Marie Laveau cast her St John's Eve rituals."

"St John's Eve?"

Antoine nodded. "You know how New Orleans is, like, the birthplace of Voodoo in America? Well, St John's Eve is maybe the most powerful night on the Voodoo calendar. Supposed to be the night before John the Baptist was born."

"But that'd be more like a Christian thing though, wouldn't it?"

"Well, that's where it gets complicated. You've got to understand, Voodoo isn't just some African folk religion. Vodoun was a system of religions and tribal beliefs. Then it comes through Haiti to New Orleans, and…well, this is a Catholic town and always has been. Voodoo as it's practiced here includes a pretty big spoonful of that. Anyway, legend has it these rituals Laveau did were quite a sight. Thousands and thousands of people turning out to see 'The Voodoo Queen' do her thing. Snakes, skulls, knives, drums, runes on the ground, howling and screaming. Even possession if you believe that. The whole works. You stay here a while and you'll hear all about her. Of course, they're pretty sure now it wasn't *her* who did the big rituals on St John's, but her daughter."

"So, there was more than one?"

"Only two that practiced, if I remember right. But a lot of people came to 'Marie Laveau,' either the first or the second, looking for divinations, readings, advice about their problems, blessings on marriages and pregnancies, you name it.

Especially the rich white folk. They believed in her. Said she knew everybody's business and everybody's heart. Said she could be in multiple places at once. That she'd been gifted by the spirits."

"Huh. Do you believe that?"

"My momma's aunt sure did. Right up until she died. Her family's been in New Orleans since before the Civil War. They were free Creoles, just like Laveau. That's the only real reason I know about this stuff. Aunt Desiree took it real serious. Me? I think if Marie Laveau was half the Voodoo Queen they say, that she knew how to listen while she cut rich folks' hair, *and* that she had a little army of daughters who looked just like her. You do the math."

Kyle laughed. "Kind of a skeptic, ain't you?"

"I've had about as much religion as I can stand. But Aunt Desiree? Like I said… Anyway, I do think a person can make themselves believe just about anything, and yeah, maybe that can manifest as something real. So, I can't exactly say no, it's all bullshit. I mean the fancy, theatrical stuff—"

"More theatrical than skulls and snakes? Like what?"

"Like, actual spells. Just some good old-fashioned New Orleans bunk. Gives the tourists some of that good old local lore they came to hear. Like some crazy ass story about this fella who Laveau got so worked up one Saint John's that he just vanished or burned up or something. Some say he was taken by the spirits. But even Aunt Desiree thought he'd just gotten whacked out on whatever juice they passed around at those rituals, got too near the Bayou and drowned himself. Weren't no way they were going to try to pin it on Laveau, but as luck would have it, at some point during the celebrations, a stranger had happened upon their Saint John's Eve. Now, I'm sure you can imagine what happens when a large crowd of suspicious folks notice somebody's missing, and some outsider just *happens* to appear. They had that poor bastard strung up and swinging in Jackson Square not three days later, denying to his last breath that he even knew the guy who'd disappeared."

"Jesus."

"Relax," Antoine laughed. "Like I said, this is just the colorful shit folks make up. I'll take you to one of the real shops in the Quarter if you want, where the locals get their supplies. Not one of the tourist traps, though they can be kind of fun too, just for a look."

"Supplies? Wait, you mean people still do that shit?"

"Of course."

Kyle shuffled his feet, downing some more of his drink. "I don't know. Still kind of freaky, ain't it?"

"Voodoo's just another religion. Believers turn to it, pray to its spirits, make offerings, ask for blessings, just like any other. Remember, lots of Catholic influence. Relax, Shreveport. Ain't nobody gonna hex you with it. Hell, on the contrary. Most of the spirits are protectors. They can get pretty damn nasty if you try to use them in anger or against somebody. That's what Aunt Desiree told me anyhow. Something to do with every spirit knowing the heart of the one who calls upon its magick, and if you abuse their gift or hurt an innocent with it? They got a way of making that magick go awry. Of making their displeasure known in the nastiest way possible. So, don't go thinking you're gonna go pick up a Voodoo doll to get back at your daddy or nothing. But hell, we can go today if you're curious."

Kyle shivered, finishing off his drink and tucking the empty bottle into the pocket of his shorts. "I'll think about it."

Antoine laughed at him again. "Think all you want, Shreveport. I don't think they're going anywhere. And neither are you, right?"

Their eyes met once more, the space between them closing before Kyle even realized he was moving.

"Right," he said with a grin, accepting Antoine's kiss. "No hurry at all."

MARC

Marc double-checked the apartment number on his phone before ringing the ancient, rust-covered buzzer. The listed names were so faded, he wondered if any of their owners could still be alive, much less still in residence. Not so much as a faint buzz acknowledged his attempt, so he tried again. Nothing. The guy had said two, right? He checked one more time. He had it right. Apartment three at two o'clock.

Of course, it had all been too good to be true. The job. The offer of a place to live from one of the strippers, right in the Quarter with cheap rent. He had no idea if the guy was even home, or if the offer was the product of booze or drugs or who knew what else. Did he even have the guy's real address? Sure, that'd be fuckin' funny. Send him to some stranger's house. Maybe even to bother the guy's ex. Hi-fucking-larious.

He heard the gate's latch give way as he pushed it. Great security!

Marc was halfway up the rotting wooden stairs before he could think about it. He could just make out the faded number three painted on the ugly green door. Well, the guy had warned him it was cheap. Judging by the voice he could hear inside, he had the right place. The door felt solid enough when he knocked.

"Jesus! Hold on, will ya?"

The door abruptly opened, wiping away his doubts. Marc saw the same man he'd seen at the bar. Long, sinewy body, pale skin highlighted with a number of colourful tattoos. The leopard down one arm, the snake down the other, and the grinning skull below his navel. But while the cocky, half-naked boy who'd drifted toward him from the bar had been all sex and charm, that same guy now stared him down with obvious annoyance.

"What the fuck do you want?"

The voice hit him like a punch across the jaw.

"Uh…I'm Marc, remember? You said to come by, check out the room?"

The guy's face didn't budge. Even the damn cigarette that hung from his lips didn't move, until finally… "Oh yeah! Shit, man. Marc! Right. I'm sorry. Gimme five minutes."

Marc nodded, stepping inside. The apartment's interior matched the broken gate well enough. Four empty bottles of cheap whiskey sat on an equally cheap-looking kitchen table draped in a faded Confederate flag. A half full ashtray, into which his prospective roomie dropped his cigarette, hung for dear life to the table's corner. The room was otherwise pretty bare, with the exception of an average-sized TV and gaming console on a low coffee table against the wall. He couldn't make out what the console was, but the coffee table looked even nearer death than its taller, Confederacy-sworn colleague. Crumpled clothes covered one side of a thick mattress on the opposite wall, while a couple of thrown-back sheets draped the other. But that was it, give or take. It made enough sense to Marc, if the guy had just come by the place through a friend.

"Yeah, you hear me now?" The guy continued his phone conversation, holding up two fingers to signal he wouldn't be long. "Okay, good. So, you can hear this. *Fuck you*, asshole, and fuck that gook you—no, no, you fuckin' listen to *me* now..."

Marc tried to ignore most of the conversation as he wandered the room, trying to get a better fix on the stark apartment and its occupant. The kitchen was tiny, with an ancient looking fridge, a few beer cans, and three more empty bottles. Shit. Was the guy collecting or what? What he could see of the bathroom was just as pokey.

Wait. Where was the other room?

"No, no, no, no. Fuck that shit! Fourteen hundred, Lou. No, you lousy prick, it always was fourteen hundred. You're fuckin' lucky I'm still lettin' you have that. I don't fuckin' care. Shake it out of his scrawny ass if you got to!"

Marc opened his mouth, only to shut it again when he gestured at him to wait.

"No, shut your goddamn mouth and listen," he said. "You think I'm here handin' out fuckin' favors? Fourteen hundred. This week. Don't care how. Else I'm gonna come shake that shit out of you. Oh yeah, *that* part you fuckin' understand!"

Marc winced as he tossed his phone down on the table with a loud clunk.

"Sorry 'bout that." He crossed into the kitchen, pulled out another whiskey bottle and cracked it without offering Marc a sideways glance. "Not exactly a great first impression I know, but this guy..." He poured a glass, then held the bottle aloft, offering it to Marc.

"Huh? Ah, yeah, sure."

"Hope you like it neat. Icebox is broke."

He felt the dancer's cold fingers brush the back of his hand as he accepted the drink, more welcome than he wanted to admit. His palms were sweating.

"Like I said, this guy... Some people just take advantage, you know?"

Marc hoped a sip of whiskey would make the silence less awkward. The cheap shit felt like razors sliding down his throat.

"So anyway, this is it. I guess you took a look around already?"

"Yeah," he finally got out. "Kind of. Umm—"

"Water's good," the dancer continued, turning on the kitchen faucet to prove his point. "I don't cook or nothin', so the stove's all yours if you can get it goin'. Toilet's backed up a couple of times, but I got some stuff for that."

Marc swallowed, lifting his glass again. The drink burned no less than it had the first time. He tried not to stare at the bed. Another glance at the Confederate flag showed up the big tear down its centre.

"That's the asshole's," Ash explained. "Can't say why he left it. Fuckin' idiot."

"It's fine, I just—"

"You just what?"

"Where...where would I sleep, exactly?"

"Huh? Oh...ah...." Ash flashed him the same grin that had sucked him in the night they'd met. "That's why it's only three fifty. Each, I mean. That's cheap as hell for the Quarter, man."

"Yeah, but... Sorry, this was a bad idea."

"Awww, don't you worry, handsome. I can keep my paws to myself."

Marc took another sip, almost finishing the drink. He didn't care about the taste or the burn any more.

"You got much stuff?"

"No," he admitted, thinking of his gym bag and five sets of clothes that hadn't been washed in weeks.

"Well, that's good. Building ain't exactly big on closet space."

"Hey, look, Kellan?"

"Ash, man. Ash. Kellan dances on the bar. We've all got another name for that. You got me?"

"Sure, I got you. Ash, man, I don't know if this is a good idea."

Ash frowned, downing the rest of his drink and setting the glass down on the table with another loud clunk. "What the hell's wrong? Told you it was cheap. And hey, this ain't permanent or nothin'. Hell, if things work out, we could even get ourselves a whole new place. What do you say?"

"It's not the place."

"So? What's…" He trailed off, the cocky smile returning to his lips as he pushed his shoulders back, flexing his modest pectorals. "Hey listen, stud." He flopped a colourfully tattooed arm around Marc's shoulder before Marc could move. "You know when I said I'd give you that dance for free, that was just business, right?"

"Dance?" A shell-shocked moment later, Marc remembered.

"Hell, I was just bein' flirty. That's the job, man. It don't mean nothin'."

"So…you're what? Gay? Bi?"

The stale scent of cigarettes and whiskey on the guy's breath shouldn't have turned him on this much.

"Gay for pay, baby," said Ash, taking back his arm and sauntering over to the pile of clothes. He plucked out a bright red tank top and slipped it over his head. Against his blonde hair and the dark blues and greens of his snake tattoo…damn. "Yourself?"

"Same," Marc lied, hoping the guy didn't notice his boner.

"Because that don't bother me or nothin', just so we're clear."

"No, I mean ah…we're clear. It's cool."

"Awesome," the dancer extended his hand, squeezing Marc's before bringing them both up to his chest. "You're a fuckin' life saver, man. Hey, I gotta head out. Bring the money by the bar tonight, all right? It's three fifty. I'll set you up with some keys, then just bring your stuff over whenever."

"Umm, Ash?"

"Hey, gives me some time to clean up a bit, maybe see if I can get that stove workin'."

Marc stared at the open door and the grinning young blond jock propping it open. His new roomie.

What the hell had he just signed on for?

*   *   *

Marc hadn't exactly been ready to take Ash's word for granted. Still, the keys were waiting for him at the bar that night. Three hundred and fifty dollars later plus another five dollars to the door, he'd had them in hand, along with another drink, courtesy of his new roomie, and a gym bag stuffed with whatever he'd managed to cram in before getting on the bus. He couldn't say why he'd chosen to stay and watch the show, or to watch Ash, not that the guy had made much effort to talk to him. He'd told himself he had to watch the dancers, learn how they moved, and more importantly, how they worked the clientele. But even if that had been true, his eyes were fixed on Ash, save a few glances at the muscular Latino guy, which he could only put down to natural male reflex.

He could have picked a worse role model. Ash looked like he was genuinely having fun up on the bar, hoovering up tens and twenties from admirers once he stepped down to the bar floor. After watching Ash for about half an hour, Marc noticed something else. The guy was hard. Or maybe he was just…No! Hell no! Ash had been walking around, boned up under his shorts for any starving daddy with enough cash to see. Gay for pay? Hell, Marc wasn't sure he could pull off that trick, and he was the genuine article. Still, the few times Ash had come over to him, saying hi, offering to take his bag out back, and especially nuzzling his neck, a stunt he guessed was intended to shake loose a few more tips, his manhood hadn't exactly ignored the call. Just like it wasn't now they were in bed.

He'd been laying there for over an hour, listening to his roommate's unconscious breath, watching his body gently rise and fall, still damp and acrid with sweat. Ash hadn't warned him he slept naked. A couple of thin sheets were all that concealed what Ash had been teasing all night. Marc felt his stomach tense as Ash rolled onto his back. He inhaled another wave of the scent as his sleeping bedmate tossed an arm up above his head and was still once more. He gently bit his bottom lip as his gaze worked its way down Ash's reclining arm to his pit and over his gently defined chest, pale blue in the light that came through the shutters. Swallowing, Marc reached down and squeezed the tip of his own dick. He would have taken care of things right now if he'd been sure it wouldn't wake Ash. Sure, that would have gone well. Especially now he'd claimed to be straight.

He brought the rest of his fingers around the shaft, squeezing harder, until a sharp intake of air escaped him. His heart leapt in his chest as he heard Ash's quiet moan. He instantly let go of his cock, tensing every muscle, waiting for…what? What did he expect to happen? That Ash would freak out? Why should he? Marc was just another horny dude who needed to take care of himself from time to time. Why should their sharing a bed change that?

He had just relaxed again when Ash's other hand slipped under the sheet. He didn't need much imagination to know its destination. Marc's heart was slamming inside his chest again. Ash's eyes were still closed, his breath steady as it had been for the past hour. The gentle rise and fall of his chest, his scent, the way the muscles of his stomach gently contracted and expanded with each breath. Nothing had changed. He was asleep. The guy was jerking off in his sleep.

Marc swallowed, trying to relieve the dryness in his throat as he watched. He couldn't remember ever watching another man's body so closely, every faint twitch of every muscle as Ash pleasured himself. The sound of Ash's breath deepening, a faint sigh escaping him as he paused his movement, then kept going. Marc's fingers returned to his own cock, gently stroking in time with the man beside him. Back and forth, until the sheet slipped. And there was Ash's perfectly hard cock, swelled in his hand, gently rocking back and forth as Marc watched.

Had the sheet fallen on its own? Or had Ash pulled it down?

The guy had been teasing Marc all night. Nuzzling him, putting his arm around him. Sure, he'd said he was straight. They both had. Then they'd both gone to bed naked with another guy. Now they both had hard-ons.

Marc reached out, tentative and scared as he'd ever felt in his life, stopping so close to Ash's stomach he could feel it brush the tips of his fingers each time the guy breathed in. Considering the sweat Ash had worked up, his skin felt surprisingly cool and dry now. But the movement didn't slow. Didn't change. Marc relaxed his fingers against Ash's body, the feeling sending a jolt straight to his cock. Had he still been touching it, he might have come then and there. He slowly let his fingers drift down Ash's side, finally resting his hand on the guy's leg. His heart leapt again as a sharp hiccup of breath interrupted Ash's steady sleep, and the guy's hand left his cock, flopping off the side of the mattress. But he remained asleep. Remained hard. Marc knew he should let go. That he should just go into the bathroom, jerk off, then come back to bed and pass out. But the heat of Ash's balls felt too good against the back of his fingers. He hadn't even realized he'd brought his hand up so high. Ash's cock practically fell into his hand.

Ash stirred again, emitting the same little moan Marc had heard before as Ash had begun jerking himself. He wanted this. It had been obvious from the moment they'd met. 'I'd give you a dance for free?' Just bein' flirty, huh?

Bullshit.

Bullshit, because of the way Ash was moaning and thrusting his cock into Marc's hand. Bullshit, because of the way the guy moved his leg so the inside of his thigh brushed against Marc's bare skin. Bullshit because of the way he didn't flinch when Marc spread a hand over his muscular stomach, happily continuing to receive Marc's touch, then just as happily receiving Marc's tongue.

Inhaling Ash's scent, welcoming the faintly sour taste of his skin, the heat of the cock head as it pushed along his tongue, leaving a trail of sweet precum in its wake...it only pushed Marc to go deeper, harder, taking Ash's manhood down to its hilt as he spread his fingers across the smooth curves of the guy's abs, his other hand gripping the inside of Ash's thigh. Another faint groan escaped Ash as he brought up his hand to grab Marc's wrist. Marc almost dropped Ash's cock. He felt every muscle in his body tense, ready to be pushed away or worse. But Ash continued to sigh, pushing his cock deeper between Marc's lips.

"Don't stop," he murmured, eyes still closed.

Marc didn't, wrapping his tongue around Ash's shaft once more and drawing deep, ignoring the ache in the base of his own erect cock as he focused on Ash. Ash moaned again, gripping Marc's arm tighter. The sudden release of his thick stream caught Marc off guard. He jumped back as Ash's body jerked several times, ejaculating over his stomach and chest. Feeling the heat of drops on his hand, Marc pulled Ash tighter into him again, licking the shaft clean. But it was too late. Cum

CHRISTIAN BAINES

now covered Ash's taut body. Marc sat back, giving Ash some space as he took his own cock in hand and started to jerk off.

His bedmate's eyes peeled open, fixing on him in the dark. "What are you doing?"

Marc froze, his cock still in his hand, as Ash's expression hardened. The man's gaze moved from him to the river of semen running down that body, which only a moment ago had been so responsive to Marc's touch.

"Nothin'," he answered. "I'm not doin' anything."

"Like hell it's nothin'," Ash shot back. "What did you do to me?"

"You…it seemed like you wanted it. You told me not to stop."

"Like fuck!"

"You did. I heard you!"

"I was dreamin', you freak!"

Marc sat perfectly still, just focusing on his breath as he returned Ash's stare. He knew this was bullshit. Ash hadn't been asleep. He'd known exactly what he was doing. He'd wanted it. But what could he do now? Call Ash a liar? Hell, the spray of cum across the guy's stomach was doing a fine job of that already.

"Yeah? Looks to me like it was a pretty good dream."

Ash was up from the mattress like a daemon, shoving Marc hard in the chest and sending him sprawling across the floor. "What's that supposed to mean, faggot?"

Marc stared at the man who'd been nothing but inviting charm and sex up until now. In total control, tempting others with his handsome face, beautiful body, and cock. Now, exposed and humiliated, he was royally pissed off.

"Answer me!"

Marc swallowed his fear, resting a hand on his gym bag, still packed with all his stuff. "Go to hell." He snatched it up, along with the few clothes he'd left around the apartment. Ash's firm hand suddenly gripped his shoulder, pulling him back and shoving him up against the front door. He winced as Ash pressed his strong forearm pressed into Marc's chest.

"Answer me, cocksucker!"

A dozen or more answers crossed Marc's mind. Ash had liked it. Pushed harder when he could easily have pulled back. He'd draped himself over Marc all night...Fuck! Ash *had* pushed down the sheet. He'd wanted it, and Marc had provided. End of fucking discussion. Still, he knew he had to choose his words carefully.

"What were you dreamin' about?"

"What?"

"I said, 'what were you dreamin' about?'"

Confusion crossed into Ash's frown as the strength in his arms wavered. For a moment, they just stood, staring at one another breathing heavily, until Ash let him go, turning his back and stalking off.

"*Fuck*!!!" Ash brought his fists down hard on the flag-draped table.

Marc quickly found his jockstrap in the pile of clothes he'd been able to salvage and slipped it on. Gay, bi, or gay for pay, what the hell did it matter? The guy was fucking nuts.

"I'm sorry," Ash said.

For a moment, Marc just stared at the naked figure, still heaving with each breath in the moonlight. The voice had been Ash's, but unlike Marc had ever heard it. Quiet and uncertain, asking forgiveness instead of just throwing out an empty apology and expecting it.

"What?"

"I said, I'm sorry." A hint of anger had returned to Ash's tone, but Marc couldn't say whether it was directed at him or something else. "I just get...confused sometimes."

"*You're* confused?" Marc challenged, staring at the cum-covered jock. He tensed as Ash squared his shoulders again, his fists clenching. But nothing followed. Instead, Ash picked up a t-shirt and wiped the seed from his body before tossing it aside.

"Do you want water or anything?" Ash asked, his voice still quiet.

Marc shook his head, watching as Ash headed for the kitchen without waiting for his answer. He knew he should leave. Knew he should grab the rest of his shit, shut the door behind him and not look back. No. Forget his shit. He had to go. He couldn't give Ash another chance to freak out on him like that. He even had his hand on the goddamn door handle.

The thing wouldn't budge. He'd locked it. The goddamn psycho had locked him in!

"Marc? I said, you want anything?"

Yeah, the key, asshole! He couldn't say it aloud. His voice had seized up. He grimaced as the cold from the door handle seemed to invade his hand, passing through his knuckles and through his wrist, finally wrapping itself around his forearm where it stayed like an icy ring pressing into his soft, pale flesh. If Ash was saying anything now, he couldn't make it out. What the fuck was this? The cold…like a ring of fog had pressed around his arm. It was starting to hurt.

"Marc?"

He startled, turning back to see Ash sipping a glass of water, holding another out to him. He took it, not realising until he was gulping it down that the cold pressure was gone.

"You okay?"

"Yeah, I guess," he murmured, finishing the water.

"I…I'm real sorry, man."

"Yeah, you said."

"No, I mean I'm sorry for lyin'."

"Lyin'?"

"I…I wasn't asleep, all right? That what you wanna hear?"

"Whatever, man," Marc scoffed, picking up one of his t-shirts and slipping it over his head. "I should just go."

"No, I don't mean...shit."

"Hey, will you just unlock the door? I don't think this is gonna work out. I'll find my own place."

Ash frowned at him, confused. "Unlock the...What do you mean, unlock it? Just turn the knob, man."

"It won't move. Look, this ain't funny, all right?"

"I ain't tryin' to be funny," Ash spat back, grabbing the door handle and turning it effortlessly, letting the light stream in onto his pale, naked chest. He grabbed the outside handle and jigged it a few times, just to prove his point. "See? Locks automatic on the outside, never on the inside. Nice and easy. I thought I showed you that?"

"No, you didn't, and it wasn't movin' just now, damn it."

"Well, then you were movin' it wrong, because it works just fine."

Marc grabbed his bag, gripping it so tight he felt his fingernails against the flesh of his palm. Damn it. It *had* been locked. He knew it. Ash had pulled some sly shit to make him feel a fool.

"Marc?" His voice was quiet enough to make Marc pause his packing. "Did you hear what I said?"

"Yeah, I heard you, it's not fuckin' locked."

"Not that! About lyin' to you, about bein' asleep. I knew what you were doin'. I shouldn't have pushed you. That was not worthy, Marky. I'm sorry."

"Okay," Marc muttered, picking up his bag, still full with most of his clothes. "Fine, whatever. Apology accepted. I shouldn't have... Maybe I just got you mixed up. Look, this isn't a good idea. You're gay for pay. I get it. I'm gonna go."

"No, stay, damn it." Ash interrupted, shutting the door with a loud bang. "Jesus, what've I gotta do? Spell it out? I liked it, man. *I liked it.*"

Marc swallowed his nerves once more, gripping his bag tight as Ash sauntered over to him, not the same way he had at the club but just as seductive. Marc couldn't help but drink in Ash's face as he stopped just inches away from the light that shone off Ash's golden hair, to those bright blue eyes, the sharp cheekbones and jawline, all the way down that lean body to the perfectly shaped cock that hung a good seven or eight inches beneath a soft thatch of blond hair. He barely felt Ash's hand on his shoulder.

"Look, man, if you want to fool around, just keep it our secret, all right?"

Marc scoffed, then instantly tensed as he noticed the flare of Ash's annoyance.

"All right, all right. You don't have to if you don't want it. I just... hell, I don't want you to go."

He focused on Ash's eyes, determined to find the hidden agenda. The lie of a pretty Quarter hustler who a few hours earlier had sworn his flirting and fooling around had meant nothing. But then, weren't those same words on the table now? Fooling around?

It sure hadn't felt like fooling around when Ash had slammed into him.

"I need you, man. I need a roomie and maybe a guy I can trust with certain things."

Marc tried to ignore the brush of Ash's fingers as they lifted his shirt. He failed, or his cock did at least, rising with the same attentiveness it had shown Ash all night.

"You need somebody to show you the ropes. Help you out with dancin'. Hell, do you know this town at all?"

He shook his head. That was one question he had a sure answer for.

Putting his other hand on Marc's shoulders, Ash finally smiled. "Tell you what. You stay here tonight. You still wanna go tomorrow? I ain't gonna stop you."

He couldn't find the lie or deception he'd been looking for in Ash's eyes. He couldn't exactly say why he still wasn't freaked out as hell, or why he dropped his bag and put his hands around Ash's waist, letting his forehead rest against his roomie's just for a minute. But what the guy said made some sense. He couldn't just go running off into the night. Besides, Ash had explained what had happened. So, neither of them were quite as gay for pay as they'd said. So what? And there was something almost familiar about the way Ash smiled at him. He didn't trust the guy. Didn't even like him in a lot of ways. But he felt like he understood him. Something in the two of them connected, and, hell, Ash had a point about how much they needed each other, at least for the time being. At least for tonight.

Marc eased himself out of Ash's grasp and nodded.

Ash's grin grew wider as he backed off toward the mattress. "Well, great. Then come back to bed, you crazy fuck. I got you a shift on the bar tomorrow."

He almost laughed. No, he didn't know what had compelled him to stay. But as he pulled the sheet up once more, listening to Ash's steady breath, not daring to touch the man again for fear of pushing his good luck, he barely noticed the weird ring that had bruised up so nice on his forearm. Right where he'd felt the cold pressure before. He guessed what the folks back home had told him was true. For better or worse, New Orleans changed people, in ways they couldn't begin to expect.

KYLE

"Yeah, you'll do fine. Get down here." The grizzled looking guy behind the bar tossed a dishcloth into the sink.

With a nervous swallow he hoped wasn't too obvious, Kyle lowered himself and nimbly hopped down off the bar, landing between two bar stools.

"And don't let me catch you doing that shit either. Bars get wet, smart guy. They get slippery." He pointed at the end of the semi-circular bar, which ended at both ends in a short flight of steps to the bar floor. "Stairs up, stairs down. No exceptions. We ain't offerin' insurance here."

"Got it. Sorry."

"All right, all right. So like I told you, it's twenty bucks a night to cover your space. Best to see it like you don't work for us. You work for yourself. Keep track of your tips and report 'em at the end of your shift. Don't worry, they're yours to keep over and above your twenty. Boss just likes to know what's pouring through the place, that's all."

"Umm, sure. I guess that's okay."

"All right, cool. And if one of these guys wants to take you out of here? Two rules. One, you do not leave before your shift's done without asking me, and it's no sure thing we can let you go. We got a timetable here. Second, and most important, if somebody takes you out? We don't know nothin' about it. What you do, what you charge, or what trouble you get into once you go out that door is not our problem. Understood?"

"Hey, woah. I…I ain't into that. I mean, they don't expect, like…I'm just here to dance, you know?"

"Yeah, yeah, calm yourself down. Dancing's all we need you to do. You'll get the hang of it. When can you start?"

A short blond guy with a deep, muscle-packed tan pushed past, clipping Kyle in the shoulder with a gym bag.

"Later, Dan," the guy said, handing over a piece of paper.

"Goodnight," the bartender said, running his eyes over it. His brow darkened. "Hey, wait a second."

The muscle dude yawned, stretching out a pair of biceps that bulged from an olive-green polo shirt before cracking his neck to both sides. Standing there in just his briefs and trainers, rubbing the shoulders he'd once thought to be pretty athletic for a guy of his build, Kyle suddenly felt as skinny as a seven-year-old.

"Alex, you holding out on me again?"

The muscled guy lifted his arms in a wide shrug as he backed toward the door. "Man, you want 'em to tip more, you get 'em drinkin' more. Ain't exactly rocket science."

"Yeah, yeah," the barkeep muttered. "Get out of here."

Kyle waited for the guy to leave before piping up again. "You want me to dance on the bar next to *that*."

The barkeep shrugged. "Up to you, kid. Got a slot open tomorrow night if you want it."

"Uh…" Fuck. Fuck, fuck, fuck. Could he really do this? He could dance, sort of. But what about the rest? What about when a dance wasn't enough? The stuff the bar didn't want to know about? Even if Antoine didn't freak out about him dancing, he'd sure as fuck—

61

"Hello?" The bartender snapped his fingers twice in Kyle's face. "Tomorrow. *Mañana.* You in or out?"

"Yeah...yeah, I'm in." Fuck it. He needed cash, and he needed it soon. "Like, eight?"

"Hah! That's cute, farm boy. You play up that shtick, and you'll do all right. No, dumb ass. Eleven 'til three. Peak time on a weekend. I got some of the better guys on then, so you can see what they do. You'll do fine. Now get dressed and get out of here. I got to close up."

Kyle scooped his jeans up off the floor and slid into them before slipping his t-shirt on, relieved to no longer be so exposed as another one of the dancers came emerged from the red curtain at the back carrying a small paper.

"See ya, Dan," the guy called, tossing his paper on the bar.

"Jesus, are you still here?"

"Awww, you know y'always miss me."

"Sure, sure. Fuck off."

The guy's voice was far too familiar, but it wasn't until the dancer was staring him in the face that Kyle recognized him as the guy who had tried to pick him up in the bar with Antoine. The dirty blond hair, the delicate lines of his nose and jaw, the high cheekbones which belied the misshapen top tooth that emphasized the guy's cocky grin.

"Well, will you look who it is?"

"Jesus Christ," Kyle muttered.

"Hey, don't be like that."

"You ladies want to take it the fuck out of my bar?" the bartender snapped. "Go on, get."

Kyle left, not saying a word, trying to ignore the asshole following way too close behind. His temper lasted almost a full block before he turned. "Why you followin' me now?"

"Just my way home, princess."

"Well, fuck that. Go some other way or the other side of the street or somethin'."

"I might have told you the same thing. Though I was gonna say it nicer."

"What's that supposed to mean?"

The blond guy shook his head, taking out a cigarette and lighting it before offering the pack to Kyle, who waved it away. "Three thirty in the a.m.? Ain't nobody but you and me on the street, and you're just strollin' along, all these cars parked along the curb."

"So?"

"*So*, you want to be walkin' on the other side of the street where nobody's parked. That way, no son of a bitch hidin' behind a bumper is gonna jump out in your face and—" he drove his fist into his palm so fast, Kyle jumped.

Kyle glanced at the other side of the street. Well lit. No cars. He could see the guy's point. "Why are you telling me this?"

He shrugged, muscles flexing in his thin, wiry shoulders under the flimsy white cotton of his tank top. "You seem like a nice enough guy. When I saw you at Oz that time—"

"What? What about that time?"

The guy's mouth split into that same grin again. "Got a short fuse there, don't ya?"

"Thanks for the tip," Kyle huffed, quickly scanning the street before stepping out between the cars to cross.

"All right, all right," the guy said, grabbing hold of his hand. It was a lot softer and dryer than Kyle had expected. Maybe it was the humidity or just the guy's smarmy attitude, but he'd expected it to be damp and clammy somehow. "I was an asshole that night. But don't go gettin' mad about it. That other guy was kinda cute. Maybe I was a bit jealous."

"You called him a goddamn nigger."

"Not to his face."

"What the fuck difference does that make?"

"All right, all right. You're right." He let out a long, silent breath through his teeth, raising his hands in open, symbolic surrender. "That was not worthy. If he's your friend, I'm sorry, all right? I. Apologize."

The gesture just pissed Kyle off all the more. "*Thanks for the tip,*" he muttered again, not caring if the idiot heard. He'd reached the opposite curb before the guy spoke again.

"I saw you dance."

"What's that?" he asked over his shoulder.

"I said, I saw you dance."

"Yeah? Great. You can give me a dollar."

"Don't imagine I'll be doin' that. Don't imagine hardly anybody will."

Kyle felt his fists clench. This guy…

He was across the road before he could gather his thoughts. Was he looking to get laid out? Kyle might have taken a swing already if…goddamn it, he was hard. Why the fuck was he hard? The guy was smiling at him now, almost seeming embarrassed as he glanced down, dimples deepening, the stronger lights only emphasizing his high cheekbones. When he looked Kyle in the eye again, the smile seemed almost sincere.

"You're way too tense up there, man."

"Guy behind the bar said I was fine."

"Yeah, Dan talks a lot of shit. You had him dreamin' about gettin' his dick wet the moment he laid eyes on you. He likes you pretty farm boy types. Besides, he's got a hell of a time tryin' to keep guys on. Lot of no shows, if you get—"

"What's your goddamn point?"

The guy looked away, his smile never wavering.

"What? You're sayin' I suck? That's your point. I fuckin' suck, basically."

"Awww, don't be sore. So what? Did you think you were gonna be hot shit your first time up?"

Kyle seethed, gritting his teeth as he turned and started walking. Damn fool. Risking losing Antoine, even, and for what? A few bucks stuffed down his jock from guys wanting a peep at his johnson? All the while surrounded by guys twice his size who could dance better? No fucking thanks. Who'd he been kidding?

"Yeah, sure, keep walkin', man. Just another dumb hick, talkin' like he can hustle a big game."

Kyle spun around so fast, he thought he was going to leap on the guy right there. But that same smile stopped him dead in his tracks.

"I could help you out."

"I don't need your help."

"You sure as hell need *somebody's* help if you want to cover your spot tomorrow. You ain't gonna get two bucks down your jock if you don't chill the fuck out."

"And just how am I supposed to do that?"

The guy smiled again, tossing his head at a darkened side street. "Let's get out of the light here."

"Hey, no fuckin' way, man. Piss off!"

"Oh, I'm *sorry*. Guess I got my eye on all that cash bundled up in those empty pockets of yours. Man, you really gotta wizen up some. We're gettin' out of the light because you don't want your sexy ass—and you do have one, farm boy—shakin' out where anyone can see you for free."

Doing nothing to conceal a loud, frustrated grunt, Kyle relented. What could it hurt? He could use all the help he could get.

"You know what your problem was up there, right?" the guy continued, throwing a glance up either side of the street, making sure they were alone. "You worried too much about what Dan was gonna think of you."

"Ain't that what counts?"

"Man, it's like I told you. You had Dan's tongue out between his man titties the second you walked in. Him and a whole bunch of other guys. You just gotta pretend they ain't there. I don't mean be rude. But don't be too eager to please."

"How the fuck am I—"

"Easy there, farm boy. Just close your eyes a second."

Kyle shook his head. "This is stupid. I can't believe I let you talk me into this."

"Hey!" the guy suddenly shouted into the street. "Step right up! Come and get it! We got a cashed up white boy over here!"

"Are you fuckin' crazy?" Kyle hissed, grabbing the dancer by his singlet and pulling him close. As the back of his fingers brushed the smooth, pale muscles of the guy's chest, he instantly regretted it. He was hard again.

"Ain't nobody here but us." The dancer grinned, gently breaking Kyle's hold. The guy was pure sex, raw and walking. No way in hell was Kyle gonna compete with that. Still, if this guy could give him a few pointers... "Now close your eyes."

Kyle did as he was told. He could still feel the guy's heat, especially now he was leaning closer. Kyle felt his breath break over his shoulder.

"You were thinkin' about dancin' up there, right?"

He swallowed as he nodded.

"Right. When instead, you gotta be thinkin' about sex."

"Huh?"

"Like what do you think about when you jerk off?"

"Oh, fuck off."

"Hey! Keep 'em closed. I asked you an easy question."

"Which is none of your goddamn business."

"You don't have to tell me, you big idiot," the guy spat back. "Just think about it. Get a picture goin' in your mind. Whaddya like? Guys? Girls? Big tits? Big long black cock?"

66

"Jesus fuck! What is your prob—" Kyle's eyes sprang open again as the guy stepped closer without warning, his warmth now radiating off his own, his warm breath surprising Kyle with its sweetness.

"What about somethin' like this?" the guy asked, gently taking Kyle's hand and caressing the smooth, lean curve of his own chest muscles with it.

Kyle swallowed, trying to yank his hand away, but the guy wouldn't budge. "Get off me."

"Shhhhh. Close your eyes again. Pretend it ain't me. Anyone you want, farm boy. Captain of the football or wrestlin' team? It don't matter. Just get a picture in your mind."

Fuck it. Kyle was ready to do just about anything to shut the guy up. Swallowing once more, he thought about Antoine. The soft feel of his skin, flawlessly smooth, its darkness deepening as he imagined those small, inky nipples, smaller than the one he could feel—

"Hey! What the fuck are you—"

"Shhhhh. You're doing fine, farm boy. Trust me."

He closed his eyes again, picturing Antoine's face, the bright smile that had broken through his lips. Those dark eyes that went on forever. He felt his hand gliding over the dancer's skin again, the pull of the tank top against his wrist as the guy brought his hand down, down, sliding over the lip of... abs. Abs, Antoine didn't have. The skin felt different too. Harder than Antoine's. And its smell contained nothing of his lover's fastidiousness. Nothing of the colognes Antoine applied in just the right quantity to stir Kyle's curiosity but never make him gag. This guy smelled like work in a bar. Beer, sweat, the remnants of a cigarette, crumpled singles, and sex.

Kyle felt his fingers being guided down the faint crease in the guy's stomach. Then the flop of slightly damp cotton landing on his wrist. How had the cunning fuck managed to slip off the tank without breaking his hold? The scent was stronger now, and there was no mistaking how familiar it was. How much he'd missed it.

No way could this asshole be one of his uncle's farm guys. The dancer was his age, and his uncle's boys had always been a good ten or fifteen years older. But something about the man stirred his memory, reliving the same ache and heat that filled him when he'd seen that first guy laying in the back of his truck with a scrunched-up work shirt under his head and a spent beer can beside him. Thick, well worked arms had relaxed above his head, jeans undone just far enough for Kyle to make out his 'invitation,' as one of the guys had called it.

"You got that picture now?" the dancer whispered.

Kyle nodded, trying to ignore his boner. No, wait. Wasn't that the whole point? To feel like this? Or make other guys feel like... Fuck! Now he was all confused.

"You're over-thinkin' again, farm boy. I can tell. I asked, are you picturin' it?"

"Yeah," he finally got out. "I see it."

"Good."

Kyle felt the shudder go through him as the man's breath broke over his lips. He barely noticed the guy had grabbed his erection, sliding Kyle's hand down the rest of his torso until Kyle felt his fingers hooked into the lip of the guy's pants, resting on the tip of his moistened cock.

"I should..." he whispered. "I can't—"

He hushed Kyle again with one long, almost silent breath. Kyle licked at his dry lips, shuddering again as the tip of his tongue touched the guy's mouth. He felt the man's body heat come closer. Felt the thick shaft of the strange cock slip through his hand as he gently gripped it. He swallowed involuntarily as a drop of precum smeared his palm and they brushed cheeks.

"You want to taste that again?"

The smell of the guy's hunger drove him crazy. How long could it take? A minute? Some of the farm guys had cum in less.

"I can't," he protested again, embarrassed by the weakness of his voice.

"Shhh. You're feelin' it now though, ain't you?" The cockiness and meanness that had sharpened the dancer's voice before was gone.

He felt a hand ease down the lip of his jock, shivering again as the guy caressed it with cold fingers. A gentle moan escaped him as his cock slid smoothly into the guy's hand, and he barely stopped himself crying out as the guy's little finger brushed under the lip of its head.

"Yeah, man. That's it. That's what it's all about."

Kyle barely fought back his whimpering as the man settled his fist into a steady rhythm, back and forth on his cock. He was too distracted by the guy's scent and the cold ridges of strong fingers as they squeezed, then released his cock in a rhythm that matched his own grip on the man.

The dancer moaned as Kyle pressed his thumb into the base of his cock before taking the hint, teasing the head with his little finger.

"Fuck," the man breathed. "You learn fast, farm boy."

"Don't talk." He pushed himself forward again, enjoying the slickness of his own precum as it warmed the cold fingers. Their rhythm grew faster, the heat reminding him of the farm guys. Their taste, that grassy smell, soaked with earth, beer, and work. How he'd gripped and pulled at his own cock, harder than ever from that first salty lick. How he'd eagerly gorged himself, right down to the musky hilt of each one.

The dancer gripped him tighter, clapping a hand over his mouth as his body erupted, sending hot seed over the man. Seconds later, he felt the guy's sex emptied into his own hand, his shoulder muffling the dancer's moan.

Kyle collapsed against the wall, feeling the slender dancer's warm chest heaving against his own as each regained his breath. What had he just done? Jerked off with some stripper in the darkness of a back street? The sourness of sweat and cum clung to the air. Clung to both of them. He felt what was left of the guy's load on his fingertips.

"Whooeee! Damn, farm boy!" He eased himself off Kyle and wiped his hands on his tank before doing up his shorts.

Kyle wiped his hand off on the wall behind him as best he could and put away his now flaccid junk. He didn't have anything to say.

"That was some shit. Worth it. Totally worth it." The guy was smiling at him again. That same cockiness back in his eye. The smirk right back in place. Worth it? If Kyle hadn't understood the smirk before, he sure did now. It said just one thing. *Gotcha.*

His fist slammed into the guy's head before he'd even made up his mind to do it. The bastard let out a howl, looking up at Kyle just in time to catch another hit right below the eye.

The dancer cried out again, shielding his face. "Jee-sus! What the fuck, man?

"You stay the *fuck* away from me! You understand? You ever fuckin' touch me again, I'll kill you, you son of a bitch!"

"Fuckin' asshole! You liked it!" The guy backed off, cowering as Kyle lurched toward him one more time.

Kyle wanted to land just one more. One more swing at the guy was all he needed to…to what? He'd made his damn point. He turned his back and marched back toward the light.

"Don't you even think about comin' back to the bar, asshole," the guy cried after him. "I see you there tomorrow, you're dead. You hear me? Crazy cunt!"

In the darkness, Kyle saw the guy jump as he rounded on him again. Sure. Kyle was bigger, taller, and could probably lay the guy flat out in a second if he wanted to. But what would have been the point? His mind began eating itself as he charged through the dark streets. You liked it. *You liked it.* The truth behind those words turned his stomach. He hadn't even liked the guy.

And Antoine.

What the fuck was he supposed to tell Antoine?

MARC

Marc could barely remember that first time he'd blown Ash. Not the sweetness or bitterness or saltiness of Ash's cock, nor how the faint musky scent of pubic area sprinkled with sweat had smelled to him that first time. He'd all but forgotten how soft the inside of Ash's thighs had first seemed, covered in their light down of barely visible blond hairs so soft he could barely feel them under his fingertips. He couldn't quite remember how the firm muscles of Ash's stomach had felt under his fingers that first time either. Muscles that dozens of johns had touched and lusted for every other night. Even now, as Marc stroked them, the sensation seemed so alien, beautiful, and new. He lapped at the tip of Ash's dick, grateful for its taste and scent, the weight and warmth of it in his mouth. But even this did little to stir his memories of that first night when Ash had let Marc blow him.

He remembered some parts. *Don't stop*, and then, *wham*. Shoved hard to the floor. Choking as Ash pressed him against the front door with all his strength. *What you doing, cocksucker?*

Why hadn't he left right then and there? Had he just been desperate? Or maybe the sex was worth it. Worth the risk. Perhaps it was the danger that excited him the most.

The shaft of Ash's penis pushed through to the back of his throat. Its owner moaned with satisfaction, perhaps even appreciation, though it seemed brave to entertain that thought, even with Ash's moans affirming every smooth stroke of his tongue.

Ever since their first night, blowing Ash had brought a smile to Marc's face as unshakeable as the one worn by the bloody skull etched into Ash's stomach, floating in all its grinning, ghoulish glory above a perfect thatch of blond pubes.

His memories of the night they'd met were clearer. The night Ash had lured his nervous ass back with a drink, and they'd got to talking. The night he'd learned what a john was. He'd known then that this beautiful, hard looking blond kid was a lone wolf, like him. Now it seemed they made a good pair, in so far as you could call them that.

Ash's fingers ran through his uneven shock of brown hair as the guy moaned again.

"Feel good?" he asked, stroking the underside of Ash's balls.

"Don't talk."

His dick hardened instantly as Ash gripped his hair, then released him just as fast. Not that Ash couldn't hurt him if he was set on it. But Marc was a strong guy, too. He could handle himself, and Ash knew it. They'd had their disagreements and scrapes. But Ash had been right about one thing. They needed each other, and watching his back around Ash's temper, putting up with the bastard's games, was a small price for being that one guy Ash would drop the bullshit for and let suck him off just because he wanted it. It felt good to be trusted that much. Maybe that was why their first night felt so distant.

Ash moaned again, deeper, his eyes going wide as Marc went down on him.

Marc reached up, enjoying the steady, predictable contours of Ash's abs as he counted them off again. One, two, three, four... an eight-pack that contracted and heaved under his touch.

It sure was a hell of a step up from Ash losing his shit. Now, the guy's grin spread wide across his face as his cock speared its smooth course over Marc's tongue. Ash's inner faggot sure had grown some.

"Wait," said Ash, holding him still.

With the weight of Ash's cock still heavy in his mouth, Marc heard the click behind his left ear. The lock of his hair being raised. "No," he got out, hurriedly disengaging his mouth.

"What?" asked Ash, his knife gently touching behind Marc's ear. "Don't you trust me?""

Marc fell silent, trying not to wince as the cool blade pressed into his skin. Ash had to be holding it backward. The blade edge would have sliced into him on the first touch.

"Do you want my cock or not?" Ash asked, running a finger through Marc's hair again.

Marc's cock twitched with hunger. Anticipation. The tip of Ash's erection pushed against his lips, its warmth all the more noticeable with the cold metal at his neck.

"Marc?"

"I trust you."

Ash's steely blue eyes bathed him in skepticism through an unfading smile. "Just a bit of excitement, Marky. You know I wouldn't hurt you."

"I know. Can you put it away, please?" Marc felt the knife turn. Slowly. Deliberately. "Ash—" He flinched as the blade nicked his skin, so sharp and fast it barely hurt.

Ash was already wiping it between his fingers when he looked up. Satisfied, he dropped to his knees, leaned into Marc's neck and licked the cut clean.

"If you say so."

The stale odor of cigarette smoke hung on Ash's lips as they brushed Marc's face. Marc couldn't help the sigh that escaped him as he inhaled it. Ash's lips were on his before he realized it, the slightly sour, smoky taste of the guy's tongue breaking through to find his own. Marc shivered at the firmness of Ash's grip on his shoulders. The power in those arms flowed through the thick, corded veins. Marc sighed, scared and yet, strangely content in Ash's grip, his cock rigid.

Was it Ash's first time kissing a man who wasn't a john? Just because he'd wanted to?

As Ash gripped him again, he could feel the guy's finger, teasing the thin strip of flesh beneath his balls. No fair. No fair at all! As he fell backward onto the mattress, the thin sheet felt fresh and cool, cutting through the humidity that soaked their naked backs. Ash's cock was still hot and full, animated as it bumped against his flesh. No, his ass. Ash was lifting his legs.

"Ash?"

"Shhhh..."

Strange adoration filled those steely blue eyes. It unsettled him at first, then for one comforting moment, it seemed genuine as Ash's handsome face pitched toward him, locking them together in another kiss.

"Who do you belong to?" Ash asked again, spitting into his hand.

Marc let his hands rest on the hardness of Ash's body, where he could explore his strong back and shoulders. "You."

Ash grinned at him with perfect white teeth, sliding his moistened cock between Marc's buttocks.

"Ash!"

Ash clutched Marc's wrist and pinned it against his chest. "It's what you wanted isn't it, you little faggot? You've been wanting it for weeks."

Marc cried out as the rest of Ash's cock head slid into him. A deep moan escaped him as the rest of the shaft followed. In the split second before his mind went blank, he wondered if Ash was right. If this is what Marc had been wanting all along, from the moment he'd spied Ash's lithe, athletic shape in the bar, the first time he'd seen Ash masturbating his swollen cock beneath the same thin sheet now tangled between their legs. Right up to tonight, when Ash had rewarding his touch with a kiss, and—

"Ow!" He tensed at Ash's sudden grimace.

"I'll go slower," Ash mumbled.

"Just...get some lube, okay? And a condom."

"Got none left. You think I'm diseased or some shit? You think I let those fags fuck me without one?"

Marc swallowed.

Ash made a show of spitting into his hand and lathering it over his cock again before spearing it deeper into Marc's behind. It felt better this time. Steadier and smoother. Long, slow thrusts of Ash's beautiful cock. The shape and size of it. He could feel Ash pushing right up against his gut. The firm head pushing against parts of Marc that made him gasp, breathing deeper, yet faster, gulping down air that seemed to swell to all his nerve endings outside and in. Ash's once rough and careless touch didn't hurt any more. Now, it made him feel desired and powerful.

Ash even seemed to be enjoying it. He ran a playful finger down the length of Marc's hard, solid cock. Marc never stayed hard while he was being fucked. What was Ash...?

"Oh fuck!" He mouthed the curse right as Ash squeezed Marc's cock, releasing the orgasm that had been building ever since Ash had found his rhythm. Thick, ropes of it shot over his belly, up onto his chest, and the scars that decorated it. The outline of a veve. The icon of a Voodoo spirit, etched into his skin. Guardians of the dead, now coated in his own life seed.

It felt fucking great.

Ash stopped thrusting into him and stared at the aftermath.

"You gonna come?" Marc asked. He felt Ash shiver as he pulled out of Marc, his dick quickly losing its fat. Marc felt the tension grip his gut. "Please, Ash..."

It had been Ash's idea to fuck.

"Later," Ash grabbed a dirty white t-shirt and tossed it to Marc. "You feelin' better?"

Marc shrugged as he wiped himself down. "Yeah."

"Cool."

Putting about a foot between them, Ash lay down on the mattress. For a while, all Marc could do was stare at his back, the smooth muscles of his shoulders. Even the muscled curves of his butt. He reached out a tentative hand and stroked Ash's back, careful not to push too hard. When nothing happened, he let his hand slip down onto Ash's hip.

Ash grabbed his wrist and tossed it away, pulling the sheet up over his nakedness. "Go to sleep."

Marc rolled over to the other side of the mattress, staring into the darkness. "Goodnight, Ash."

*　　*　　*

He'd fallen asleep at least once. He may have wavered in and out of consciousness, but the sands of sleep weighing down the corners of his eyes left him no doubt.

Perhaps the man had followed him back from his dreams. Or through the simple, black silence of sleep. Now, the man sat just out of moonlight's reach, staring at him with dark, silent eyes. Marc could just make out the dark contours of his bare chest through the opening of a dusty black long-coat hanging around his shoulders. He held a walking stick in his hand, its shiny silver top the only other feature Marc could make out against the moonlit window.

Marc grumbled, closing his eyes and turning onto his back again. His head flopped back to one side, one tired eye peeling open, only to see the man standing there, still watching.

"What?" Marc whispered.

"If you want to sleep, you should sleep." The man's voice snaked its way through the darkness, whiny, high pitched, and full of mischief. It almost made Marc want to throw off the thin, hard sheet covering himself and Ash and go out. To find some blind-ass drunk john he could clip easily enough, then lose in the Quarter's darkened streets. Nothing too serious. Nothing dangerous. Just mean. Infantile. The culmination of wicked impulses that gripped him when he heard the stranger's voice.

"Are you watching me?" Marc's voice was the voice of a small child talking to a monster in his closet, so timid and quiet he could barely be sure he was speaking out loud. Ash's snoring, which he had fought so hard to block out on sleepless nights gone by, now offered a strange, grounding comfort, if only in knowing Ash was still asleep and wouldn't see him talking to some random, half-naked negro just a few feet from their bed.

Of course, Ash wouldn't see him. He'd see Marc talking to the fucking empty window. Talking in a dream. But this freak in the window was a damn fine, vivid hallucination.

The hallucination didn't budge an inch. "Watching over you, little boy."

"Watching? What's that mean?"

"Go to sleep. The time will come for you, soo-ooon."

Marc could feel the cold sweat soaking his body. He peeled away the sheet and looked down at the scar on his chest.

The figure held a bony black finger to its lips, leaning on its stick as it gently rose to its feet and moved to his side. Marc swallowed, more nervous sweat beading on his forehead as the man stood over him.

But what kind of man dressed like this?

Marc had seen the moonlight bouncing off the wavy, girlish black hair. It glinted on the dangling, crucifix earrings that shone with tacky gold. He wore bright purple panties, and the long black stockings that stretched beneath them along slender, smooth, yet powerfully masculine legs. The foul smoke from the faggot's cigar broke over Marc's face, and it took him every ounce of self-control not to cough with disgust.

Like this girly faggot could care less. He wasn't even looking at Marc now. He was looking at Ash.

"Beautiful, in his way, don't you think?"

Marc's gaze flicked over his friend. Ash had already rolled over, pulling the extra sheet Marc had vacated over himself. "I guess."

"He trusts you." The faggot's hand passed through the air above Ash's sleeping form. "It has taken time, but you have his faith. It is what you wanted, yes?"

"What the fuck's that supposed to mean?" Marc shook his head, desperate to avoid being dragged into a shouting match with some spook hallucination. "What do you want? Damn it, why am I talking to you? I'm dreaming this shit." His every word sounded mumbled and half formed, just like a man talking in his sleep.

"Ah, but that is good. Good that you do not remember or believe. You will know when the time is right."

"What the fuck do you mean by that? What time, damn it?"

The thing grinned, shining white teeth peering out from his dark face. "You have his trust. What does he have from you, little boy?"

"Have? I don't know."

"Trust? Faith?"

Marc startled as the man snatched up his stick and brought it down in one fast movement toward Ash's head. Marc caught it in both hands before he could think, straining as he held it firm, inches above his sleeping friend's skull.

The intruder's grin grew even wider. "Love?"

"Are you crazy? You could have killed him," Marc snapped, unable to deny his relief as the intruder withdrew his stick. A stick that had felt all too solid. All too real.

"That, I cannot do, little boy. Answer my question."

"Ash doesn't want my love. Fuck, man. We turn tricks together, that's all."

"Yet, you will defend him? Fight for him?"

"I... I just...."

The creature grinned at him again, backing off toward the window. "Soon, little boy. Soon, you will have everything you wanted. All that you deserve."

The insidious hand of sleep had regained its hold before Marc could watch the man go.

KYLE

Kyle didn't know why walking into a cop precinct should make him nervous. He hadn't done anything wrong. Yet looking over the wood paneling that separated the front desk from the rest of the precinct, watching the odd officer flick his gaze up at him before returning to work, made Kyle uneasy. More than a few of the other dancers at the bar had records for this or that, after all. Usually low-grade substances or hustling. Blaine had told him about the one guy who'd done time for putting his girl in hospital for three months. But whatever. None of it was his problem.

So why did the steely gaze of the plumpish blond sergeant behind the desk make him feel like he was about to be read his rights?

"Help you with something there, sir?"

Shit. She'd actually called him 'sir.'

"Umm...yeah," he said, emboldened as he approached the precinct desk. The NOPD merchandise for sale on the neighboring table seemed to mock him. Sure, plonk down twenty bucks for a t-shirt and show the world how proud you are of the Crescent City's finest. "I'm looking for some information."

"About?"

"A murder." The word was even harder to get out than when he'd rehearsed it.

"Uh-uh. You a reporter?"

"Yeah. I mean, kind of. College paper."

"Uh-uh." Her stare gave him nothing. "Which college would that be?"

"Uh...Tulane."

"Uh-uh. Really not the world's best liar, are ya? Everyone down here knows the girl who covers the precinct for Tulane—pronounced *too-lane*, just so you know. She drives us nuts half the time. Dresses a bit nicer than you, too."

"Sorry," he mumbled. Shit, what was he doing here? What did he expect them to tell him that he didn't already know, exactly? Antoine was dead. No shit. They hadn't caught the guy. Double no shit. "Sorry I wasted your time."

"Christine, I'm heading out," one of the cops called, retrieving his jacket from a line of hooks behind the desk.

"All right, see you in a bit," the sergeant replied.

Kyle waited for the man to go before shoving his hands in his pockets and turning to leave.

"Which file were you after, son?"

He paused, trying to read the woman. But she was more than making up for his lousy poker face. "Antoine Lavolier."

The sergeant let out a low, silent whistle. "I'm guessing the two of you weren't friends?"

"No. I mean yeah, yeah, we were." He bit back the details.

"All the facts we can share on the Lavolier case are a matter of public record. I can get you those. Anything beyond that remains confidential at the family's request."

"Wait, confidential? But he was murdered. That's gotta be public interest, right? It was in the papers, goddamn it."

"All right, sir. Calm down, please."

He huffed a couple more times, clenching and unclenching his fists, but he relented. Getting worked up right in front of a cop wasn't going to do him any favors. "I'm sorry."

Finally, her neutral expression broke into a frown, then a grimace that also seemed... Shit! She wasn't giving him *sympathy*, was she?

"Friends, huh?" she said before he could call her on it or turn and leave.

He just nodded.

She grimaced again. "Yeah, it was in the papers, all right. Page sixteen. That wasn't an accident. You know how they found him, right? You know what he was wearing?"

He nodded again. Of course, he knew. Antoine wouldn't have censored himself for anybody.

"Well, reporter or no reporter, you do *not* pass this on to anybody. The family paid good money to push the story back to page sixteen. They want this kept quiet."

Kyle clenched his fists again. More worried about their precious name than their only son. Assholes. Fucking rich Catholic assholes. "You gonna catch the bas—the guy, right?"

"Hopefully. Like I said, the family wants this kept quiet. But to be honest with you..."

Kyle didn't need her to finish. He could read between the lines.

"You still want me to get you those public files?"

"No. That's okay." He shoved his hands into his pockets and turned to leave.

"Three o'clock, tomorrow," the sergeant said quietly after he'd turned his back. "St Louis Cemetery Number Three. You didn't hear that here and don't go making a big show of yourself."

He turned back to her, offered just a quick smile of thanks, then left.

MARC

"Quit fuckin' countin' it, will you?"

"I'm not," he shot back, tucking the miserable wad of singles and fives deep into the bottom of his bag.

"Don't let Dan catch you doing that shit, either. Jesus, Marky! Could you at least try to make it look like these guys want you? Keep your jock full."

"This crap itches like hell." He took out another wad of crumbled bills. "Look at this shit, will you? Nothin' but singles. Ash, we got rent coming due."

"You won't be payin' for shit if Dan catches you not turnin' in your tips."

"I cover my spot."

"Yeah? Well your spot is fuckin' waiting. You were on five minutes ago. Hey, you're in luck. That fat ass nigger chick who likes you just came in. Horny bitch's tongue was practically hangin' between her tits." Ash pulled out the front of his singlet and mimicked licking madly between his hard, shallow pecs.

Marc toweled himself off, wiping the sweat off his shoulders and back, drying his pits. "Why you gotta be such an ass?"

For the first time that night, Ash's smile disappeared. It hardened into the well-practiced sneer that earned scorn from Dan and the other guys, wary discomfort from a lot of the johns, and massive tips from the sickos who got off on it. Guys turned on by a lover they knew would give them a black eye for using the word, then kiss them before they ever knew what had happened.

"Ash—"

"Listen to me, you ungrateful fuck," Ash sneered. "She got money?"

Marc said nothing, only to be rewarded with a strong forearm pressed against his throat.

"Bitch, I said, 'she got money?'"

"Yeah!" he choked. "She's got money. You know she's got money."

"That's right," purred Ash. "So you keep her drinkin', and when she slips you a five or a ten or she offers you a shot, you take that shit. When she wants to take things more private, you keep her there, and when she wants to put those big, luscious lips around that sweet white prick of yours—"

"Jesus Christ, Ash!"

"Then, when you've clipped her half a grand? Maybe all the way? When you're both fine and wet, and the smell of that big ol' black pussy's filling that room? You tell her 'next time,' then come right back to me." Ash kissed him, hard, strong and deep. No warning. No fanfare. Just the sweet warmth of Ash's tongue on his. "And we'll make ourselves a show that'd soak her dreams for weeks."

Marc was hard. He could feel it straining against his shorts. He'd broken out with a fresh sweat, precum leaking to the front of his shorts. He knew it because he could feel it, just like Ash could feel it, with his hand cupped around Marc's crotch.

"Jesus, Marky," Ash grinned, squeezing Marc's cock. "Hold it back, will you? You got four hours on shift yet."

He couldn't help the massive smile that broke across his face. He didn't know how long Ash had been dancing. But for all the bullshit the guy had put Marc through, he'd still looked after them both, in his own way. He barely heard Jimmy, the meth'd out twink call to him, "Marc? Get on the fuckin' bar, man. Dan's bitching me out."

Marc flashed Ash one last smile as he turned to leave. The same, familiar sneer was right back in place. "Ash?" he said. "I'm sorry."

Ash blew him a half-hearted kiss, expelling the smoke from a fresh cigarette. "Get the fuck out of here."

Not bothering to towel off again, Marc did.

* * *

Jimmy, Alex, and Blaine were on the bar already, grinding for the pleasure of any john that might shake loose a few bills. Blaine's fifty-megawatt grin lit up the bar as he accepted a lusty hug and ten bucks from a pair of Tulane jocks who probably, by the look of their solid biceps and trim waists, had better bodies than Blaine. Still nothing next to Alex, whose every twice-daily gym-toned muscle shone under the lights. The finished package was at that moment being enjoyed by that five-foot-nothing, white-haired actor guy who'd been coming in a lot the past couple of weeks.

Jimmy snapped his jock around a five from the black chick, who looked less and less interested as she stared at a mojito that was putting way too small a dent in her sobriety.

Marc pursed his lips. Was Dan getting stingy on the pours again? Way to fuck with their tips.

Once she caught sight of Marc though, Jimmy didn't exist. Her full, dark face broke into a massive smile as she ordered up another cocktail. Marc saw at once where the money was at.

So did Rafael.

Son of a bitch!

The woman edged closer to the well-built Cuban as he sidled up to her, not caring about the humidity raining down his unspoiled olive skin. She whooped with pleasure as his perfectly proportioned six feet of muscle, smooth black hair and cocky, testosterone-soaked machismo charm hopped onto the bar in one smooth, athletic movement.

Marc felt his stomach sink. With Rafael on shift, all the rest of them could hope for was scraps. He swore under his breath as he caught Ash shaking arms at him from the doorway, silently screaming, 'what the fuck is wrong with you, bitch?' He'd heard it aloud enough times to know the face. He huffed as Jimmy jumped down from the bar with a defeated grimace.

Fine. If they had to fight over slim pickings, he'd be sure to get his goddamn share. He leaned across the bar, almost mocking Rafael's opening moves as he smiled at the black chick.

"Hey baby!" She beamed as he recaptured her gaze. "How you been?"

He mumbled something about missing her every night or some such way over the top shit, then jumped up onto the bar.

Rafael's hand was on his shoulder before he could stop it. "Like that is it, stud?"

Catching Ash's nod in the corner of his eye, Marc tossed a sly smirk at the Cuban, which turned into a wide, playful grin as he recaptured the black chick's attention. "Like what?" He'd barely turned his back when Raphael wrapped a solid, muscle-stretched arm around his chest.

The Cuban's cologne washed thick through his nostrils, mingled with tangy sweat and the scent of a boozing john's cigarettes. "Not nice to steal, pretty boy," Rafael purred, the scent of the black chick's generously shared mojito sweetening his every breath.

Marc's back flattened against the damp, slick skin of Rafael's chest. It was smooth, just like his own, yet on the Cuban, it was all natural, which somehow made it feel more masculine. More powerful. As powerful as the arms that wrapped around him. Raphael slid that hand down his stomach toward his jock. He barely heard the black chick hollering over the thumping beats of the music, particularly as Rafael's finger brushed the tip of his cock. He was hard again. He could feel it. Could taste his precum as Rafael probed his mouth with the same curious finger. "Fucker," he sighed, feeling the firm muscles of Rafael's stomach push flush against his back.

"Awww, come on," Rafael whispered through what Marc assumed was that soul-melting grin of his. "Let's give them a real show." The Cuban's hands were on his shoulders again. Before he could move, he'd been spun around to face those endless, dark eyes, the soft, full lips, and a layer of stubble far better maintained than its appearance let on.

Marc closed his eyes, feeling Rafael's kisses brush down his chest and stomach.

The Cuban cheekily nipped the visible waistband of Marc's jock before hooking a finger into each side of it and leaning straight back, extending his body as far out as he could for every john's viewing pleasure. Not to mention Marc's.

The black chick tucked a fresh twenty into Rafael's belt before he righted himself with a killer smile.

"Come on. Let's make it look good," the Cuban whispered, flashing the same smile at Marc.

He didn't need to be told twice. Crouching down until the sweat beading over Rafael's tight snail trail was inches from his nose. He threw a hand between the Cuban's legs and grabbed the back of his belt, throwing him off balance, just for a second.

"Easy, stud," the guy cautioned him.

Marc cursed under his breath. He didn't have Rafael's rhythm, his confidence, or a fraction of his looks. But he could move his ass well enough to get whatever was clinging to it stuffed full of cash. His hips started rolling as he rose to his feet, hands sliding up the smooth muscles of Rafael's back as he went. He finally hooked them over the man's shoulders from behind, clasping hold as they ground against each other.

Rafael got the idea soon enough. Spreading his grin wide once more, he cupped his own hand around Marc's ass and held him tight in place, letting Marc lift a leg around his calf, sliding deeper against him as he descended again.

Marc kissed the Cuban's chest before hooking a hand into the front of his belt and leaning back, eyes still locked on his dance partner. He closed his eyes, savoring for a moment the whoops and hollers that filled the air, the clink of glasses placed at their feet, the feel of fresh green paper being slid into his jock before it snapped back into place, Rafael's strong hands on his body, gripping his waist and holding it firm. Marc tilted his head back, arms following until they planted down on the bar, arching his back as Rafael lifted him into the absurd bend. Upside down, he could see the Tulane jocks at the end of the bar, clapping wildly and roaring their appreciation in deep, exaggerated faux-straight guy whoops.

"Yeah!" barked Blaine from the other side of the room.

The black chick howled with delight, adding her own claps to the din.

Gently lowering his ass to the bar, Marc righted himself, grabbed Rafael's wrist and stood up to full height again. Rafael drew closer, stopping less than an inch from his face, his breath hot and inviting against Marc's lips. For just one second, a crazy idea entered Marc's head. To kiss him. To lap at those warm, beautiful lips and let the whole damn place lose its shit. Not letting go. Not pushing. Just kissing, arms around each other for hours, until...

Until Dan fired both their asses. Not happening. They were there to put on a show, and a show, the crowd would damn well get.

Marc's eyes darted over the black chick as she slammed down her tequila shot and slid the lime between her lips. He caught her coy smile as she saw him looking, her mouth showing up the lush green skin of the fruit she then spat and jammed into the empty glass. She raised her fingers at Dan for two more, flashing Marc a wicked grin.

He gyrated against Rafael a little longer, supporting himself with a hand on his shoulder and shaking his hips while the Cuban raised his thick arms, clasping the back of his head.

Marc heard the clink of the glasses at his feet, just as the black chick slipped a fresh twenty into his jock. He flashed his best smile and bent down, whispering in her ear. "Thanks, gorgeous."

"Yeah!" erupted another cry.

Marc looked up, expecting to see Blaine. Instead, Ash flashed him a wicked grin before he turned back to the husky-looking guy whose arm was around his shoulders.

"You boys thirsty?" The black chick nodded at the two fresh shots on the bar.

For what? A ten here and a twenty there? Marc suddenly had a better idea.

He pulled himself close to Rafael, pushing his face against the man's slick, damp chest, playfully biting the air just an inch or two short of the man's nipples. Rafael's natural scent almost overwhelmed him, mingling with the sweat running down his neck and biceps, into his perfectly trimmed pits. Marc pushed his tongue out and buried it inside one of those beautiful pits before anyone could stop him.

90

Rafael flinched, but soon realized where the money was at, letting Marc get to work as the whole damn bar whooped and hollered again.

Moving from one armpit to the other, enjoying Rafael's faint moans as he savored the taste, Marc felt the black chick slide a shot and a wedge of lime into his hand.

He pushed his tongue farther into Rafael's beautiful pit, tasting nothing but salty sweat from the humid night. He let it coat his tongue, resisting the urge to rub his face in it. When the scent became too overpowering, he pulled back sharply, shooting the spirit in one smooth movement. It went down fast, smooth, and easy. Top shelf shit. The black chick really liked him.

Rafael grabbed the wedge of lime from him before he could protest, squeezing it over his powerful chest, letting the juice run down the shallow gullies of his stomach and into his jock.

Marc stuck out his fat tongue and rolled it along the curves of Rafael's chest, catching every drop of juice as their audience reached frenzy. Sucking it from the lines of Rafael's abs. His nipples. The lip of the jock that teased him from just above the Cuban's belt. Everywhere it had spilled. The perfect tartness of it against the soft saltiness of the man's skin.

"Yeah!" The black chick's cry pierced over the cheers that erupted from around the bar.

Marc grinned out the corner of his mouth, licking juice from his lips and turning, grinding his backside against Rafael as they lapped up the attention and tips. Most nights, he was plenty happy to get a couple of hundred bucks in his jock. But tonight was different. Tonight was fun. No. Better than fun. It sated a need for attention. Hell, maybe even love, for his body at least.

He closed his eyes and let it surround him, barely feeling Raphael slip a hand over his hip and up his stomach. He smiled again as the Cuban tweaked his nipple, the heat of their dance warming his back. Hot breath warmed his neck, and the inviting heat of sex pushed through the back of his jock. Lips that felt strangely cold kissed the back of his neck, while the hands that encircled him worked their way down to the lip of his jock, teasing it, flicking at it, beckoning the fully swelled hard-on threatening to break free. It wasn't like anybody cared. If anything, it would double his tips. Marc let the man's heat, scent, and arousal overwhelm him as he pulled down his jock and let his cock spring free.

He was immune to the applause now, as the hands rolled smoothly over his skin, over his hips, along the crease of his ass, and down the inside of his leg, while he pumped at his erection with steady, clean strokes. They weren't supposed to be doing this, but Dan wasn't doing shit to stop them. Would Marc even listen if the man did? He felt the cold fingers stroking under his balls, another working the lip of his ass, until they squeezed together, the combined pressure more than he could take. He tried to let go of his cock too late, as white-hot juice erupted over his hand, his belly, his key strap, the bar... Only when he opened his eyes did he realize he'd missed the black chick by inches.

Rafael just looked at him, stunned.

Even in the fog of post-orgasm euphoria, surrounded by the whooping and hollering of the entire bar, whose patrons were now tossing scrunched up green bills in their direction, he could feel Dan's eyes on him, ready to ream him out for popping his cork in the open. He dived off the bar and ran, pushing a pissed-off, half-dressed Jimmy out of his way before fleeing into the night. Its thick humidity filled his lungs and clung to his bare chest as he ran, putting as much distance as possible between himself and the incriminating wayward load.

He was up St Louis and halfway over Rampart before he realized where he was, or that Rafael was on his heels.

"Hey, Marc? Marc! Where are you going, man?"

Good question. What was his plan, now the whole bar has seen him shoot his wad? Dan had to be spitting hell. And he was heading for…where, exactly? The cemetery? Dumbass. Was he trying to get himself killed?

"Jesus! Wait up, will ya?"

"Yeah, all right, stay there. I'm comin'." Marc fidgeted as he scanned Rampart Street for traffic, trotting over to his show partner, who just stared at him in disbelief. What the fuck had possessed him to do a stupid thing like that?

"Shit, man!" Rafael said, leading him back into the Quarter and a good block away from the bar before relaxing against an ornate doorway. All trace of his 'Cuban' accent was gone as moonlight caught the sweat on his dark shoulders and chest. "You want to warn a guy before you bolt? Where'd you learn to run like that? And where did you think you were going? Fuck!"

Marc shook his head, hands resting on his knees. Stupid. He should have waited. Should have tried to explain or work it out. Now, give it a day and he'd be on the blacklist of every bar in the Quarter. No dancing. No hustling. No cash. "Dan's pissed as hell, isn't he?"

"Don't worry about Dan." Rafael waved away his question. "There's more green than white on the bar right now, if you get my meaning. Unless some cop I don't know was in there tonight, I think you're cool."

A smirk formed on Marc's face as he remembered what some ex-hustler had told him one night when he was first starting out. Get to know the cops, or better yet, know what one of them likes.

Then, the smirk turned into a laugh, one that started Rafael laughing, until they were both in hysterics.

"That was…" Marc finally wheezed. "I mean, when you—"

"Hey, you're not the first to pop his cork on the clock, all right?" the Cuban got out. "Sorry to disappoint you. But man, what a scene!"

"Did you see…did you see the black chick's face? I think she thought I was gonna—"

"You nearly did. Are you on a dry spell or something? You exploded in there."

"That was your fault."

"Me? You got riled up all by yourself, stud." The Cuban laughed again, sidling closer, taking cover inside the doorway from the lights of a passing car.

The scent of the man's cologne hit Marc immediately, stronger than it had in the bar, amplified by the perspiration that coated his body. Rafael leaned back against the doorway, lifting his arms above his head, the same powerful arms he'd wrapped around Marc in the bar.

"What time is it?"

Marc swallowed, hoping it would suppress the massive boner that had sprung up inside his jock. It didn't do shit. "Almost two."

Rafael grinned as Marc adjusted his jock. "Wow. Doesn't take you long, does it? You'll be ready for an encore."

"I don't know about that." He stifled a laugh, watching as Rafael lowered a hand and hooked his thumb into the waistband of his jeans. "How about you?"

"Maybe." Rafael's grin glowed in the middle of his dark face.

Marc dove straight toward it, tasting the rum still on Rafael's lips, enjoying the warmth of the man's chest as he pulled it close to his own. The Cuban mumbled something into his mouth, only to receive Marc's tongue. Marc seized the invitation, relishing the sweetness of it as he slid his hands over the dancer's slick back.

Rafael gripped his sides with both hands, gently but firmly breaking his hold and forcing him back. The man was staring at him, all the cockiness now gone from his dark eyes.

"What are you doing?"

"I…" Shit. What had he been doing? It had felt good. That much he knew. Rafael had tasted good. "I don't know. I'm sorry. I didn't—"

"It's cool," the Cuban interrupted, raising his hands. "Just save it for the bar, yeah?"

"Yeah," Marc said automatically. "The bar. Yeah, of course. That's what I…what I meant."

The man was gone before he even finished. Marc winced, screwing his eyes tightly shut. Why the fuck had he done it? What had he expected to happen? They'd put on a show, got their cash, or more likely, Rafael had got their cash, and he'd mistaken it for what? Some kind of moment they'd had? A moment that had added his name to the dubiously honored list of hustlers who'd gone full-service porn star on the bars of the French Quarter? For a stunt that hadn't earned him a fucking dime?

When he opened his eyes, Ash was standing right where Rafael had been moments before. Standing there, staring right at him.

"What was that all about?"

Mark shook his head, pushing his way out of the doorway. He just needed to walk.

"Hey, where you goin'? I'm talkin' to you!"

"I got excited, all right?" he answered. Jesus, did Ash have to know every fucking detail? "It felt good up there."

"Oh, uh-huh? Well, it looked good, Marky. Looked real fuckin' good, 'til you freaked out and took off for the fuckin' cemetery in nothing but your jock. You tryin' to get yourself killed? What the fuck's wrong with you? You had 'em eatin' out of your fuckin' hand."

"Yeah, my fuckin' jizz soaked hand. Classy, huh?"

"Like they give a shi—will you hold still and listen to me?"

He gasped as Ash grabbed hold of his shoulder and spun him. "Hey! Chill out, will you?"

"Me? Oh, I'm supposed to chill out? Man, you get your ass back there before Dan decides to fire it, and me along with. You get me?"

He snorted, almost silently as a couple of well-dressed queens shuffled by.

"Evenin'," Ash called to them, not taking his eyes off Marc. The two strangers didn't even look up.

"Did you get my tips?"

"Get your...get... bitch, I'm keepin' your tips! Like you said, we got rent comin' up."

Whatever. He wasn't in the mood for this. Not Ash's temper. Nor his attitude. But Ash and Rafael were right about one thing. He had to go back and apologize. Maybe save his shitty job.

"So, you gonna answer me?"

"I told you. It got me excited."

"What did? Dancin'? Just dancin' with that spic got you hard enough to blow your—"

"Geeze, will you keep it down?"

"Oh, well, I'm soooo-rry!" Ash howled, letting his voice echo off the houses around them. "His royal majesty would appreciate some discretion about the fact that he slobbered all over some big brown cock this evening."

"And you're a fucking asshole!"

"Nothin' but truth though, ain't it? That fat, spic foreskin gettin' you all 'excited' and all."

"Jesus! Ash, what the hell is wrong with you?"

"You know what's wrong, you little bitch!" Ash snarled, shoving him with a loud bang against a courtyard fence. "You think I'm stupid? I fuckin' saw you. I saw everything. Hey, I expect it from that sleaze ball. But you?"

"It was just a dance, man. Jesus."

"Jesus, fuck. Will you quit lyin' to me? You were all over him. You kissed him! Fuck! Probably would have sucked him off right there, if he'd let you."

"Ash, you saw it. Up there on the bar. He wanted to show off with me. He had his hands on me."

His friend stared at him a moment, confused. "No, he didn't."

"He did! Fuck! You were watching him. He had his hands all over me. Is that what you can't stand? That some 'spic' might actually want me?"

"He didn't touch you in there, you crazy son of a—"

"I felt him, Ash!"

"Oh, you felt him, huh? Felt those big, greasy paws all over your pasty white—"

"Will you stop?"

"Stop what? I'm just givin' it to you straight, Marky. *Straight*. Like the Cuban fuck you just threw yourself at. Oh yeah! His old lady popped out a fresh little spic last month, in case you didn't know about that!"

"Ash—" he growled.

"Oh, I'm sorry! Does the truth hurt? Does the truth hurt, Marky? I know you would have sucked him, and then you would have come right back to me. Kissed *me* with a mouth full of his spic jizz."

"Fuck off!"

Marc was too blind with rage to duck the fist before it hit his jaw, sending him back into a wooden gate with another loud crack that echoed around the street. His face ached, and his cheekbone felt as if it had been driven up behind his eye. He wasn't sure if his jaw was even in place. He couldn't feel anything wrong with his teeth, as he overheard Ash muttering, pacing in the street.

"Fuck," Ash mumbled. "Fuck, fuck, fuck, fuck, man. Why do you do this to me?"

"I didn't do shit!" He cringed and cowered as Ash surged toward him, stopping just short of his face, breathing heavily.

"Fuck," Ash muttered. "That's gonna leave a mark. A mark on little Marky. Shit, why'd you make me do that?"

Marc swallowed. He could have fought. Could have argued some more, but what was the point? What could he hope to gain except a matching shiner to go with his aching jaw? "I can't go back to the bar like this. After what happened, if Dan sees—"

"Yeah, yeah. I can take care of Dan. Maybe. We need to get some ice on that. Or else your face is gonna be fucked for... Jesus!"

He watched as Ash began to walk away up the street. "Rafael," he called.

"What?" Ash answered, turning and screwing his nose up.

"His name's Rafael. Not Jesus, asshole."

After a second or two, Ash finally cracked a smile. "Okay, that's funny. That was fuckin' funny, Marky."

He rubbed the spot on his jaw. Nothing broken. He'd live. "Yeah. Yeah, real fuckin' funny."

KYLE

"Yeah, I can do them. You're not the first. On your chest, right?" She was looking at one of the pictures he'd given her, an old man kneeling with the aid of a gnarled walking stick, petting the handsome dog by his side with his free hand. The figure was naked, save for a red cloth slung over his shoulder that loosely covered him. Something about it made Kyle feel safe, like he was protected somehow.

The tattooist turned her attention to the second picture, one that Kyle knew well from where it hung in a bunch of the bars. The grinning death's head he'd mistook for Papa Legba. At least the jerks at Laveau's had set him right on that. And when Kyle had found an actual picture of old Legba, with his knotty looking cane and dog, the two had just seemed to balance each other.

"Right side? Left side?"

"Umm, left I guess."

"Which one?"

Kyle swallowed, hesitating just long enough for her to pick up on it.

"You know who these guys are, right?"

"Well, yeah. They're like Voodoo gods or somethin'."

"Kind of," the tattooist said slowly. "But Voodoo has the same god as Catholicism. These guys are more like spirits. Servants of God. And I get a lot of weekend warrior types in here—you know, frat guys or whatever—wanting permanent 'souvenirs' of the local culture. Guys who don't take two minutes to Google that shit before I stick under their skin, you know?"

Kyle just stared at her.

"Hey, that's not to say you're... It's your choice, guy. But this is the kind of stuff they ask for. That's all. You don't seem like the type."

"Do people like it?"

"Some, I guess," she shrugged. "Always somebody out there for everything, right?"

"I mean do tourists like it?"

She frowned at him, brushing a dreadlock off her face and crossing her arms. Her soft dark skin was covered in intricate designs. The foliage of a garden with thin purple flowers sprouting through it up one arm, and something that looked like computer circuitry up the other. "You planning on showing it off too many tourists?"

Was he making a mistake? No, no he wasn't. Most of the guys wouldn't have thought twice about saying what they did for a living, and nearly all of them had some kind of ink. Did he really care what this chick thought? "I dance."

"Dance?" she asked. "Ooooh, right. At the Pub? Oh. You mean at the other place."

Kyle swallowed. 'The other place?' Like the Pub was so fucking classy! "More ink? Better tips."

"I hear that. This your first?"

"No."

She winced as he showed her the Fleur de Lis on his forearm. "You know, for thirty bucks I could fix that shit right

100

up. Make it look like that asshole knew what he was doing to you."

Kyle snorted indignantly.

"I heard that. You want to look like some dime a blow-job Quarter hustler that's fine by me. Now, let's find you some real art." She pulled a large binder from under her desk and started flipping through its images. "If you want the loa, just like the pictures you brought in, you're looking at maybe one-fifty each. At least double that if you want color. I'll probably get you back two, maybe three times, but I can get you outlined tonight."

"What are you looking for?"

She flipped a few more pages and with a triumphant grin, turned the binder around and showed him the sketch. A cross, but no plain old church symbol. There were cross lines all through it with stars at the points and weird diamond shapes all around. On either side stood two small coffins, covered in crossing lines.

"Cute," Kyle said, tracing the pattern with his finger.

"I'm just giving you options, guy. You want something more authentic? This here's called a veve. Every loa's got one, and this is Samedi's. He's probably the most famous one. The cross, because he's the guardian of the graveyard, right? The loa who watches over the dead."

"Loa?"

"Yeah, that's what they're called, the Voodoo spirits. You want to stop somebody dying, or protect the soul of somebody who just died? This is your guy. Only there's not just him. There's a bunch of these guys, all playing their own, slightly different part, each with their own personality, all looking out for the dead in some way or other."

Kyle winced before he could stop himself.

"Somethin' wrong?"

"Uh, no. No, it's…" He wasn't about to tell her the truth. That he just wanted something to remind him of Antoine. To remind him of how happy Antoine had seemed, talking about his aunt, and all the history, like Marie Laveau. "It's cool. I mean the picture. I like it."

"The veve. You like it, huh? Only it's kind of big. If you want two on your chest…"

"You got the other one in there?"

"Legba? Pretty sure I do."

Kyle's breathing slowly returned to normal. Even though they'd never find out, remembering Antoine with some Voodoo symbol would probably piss off his rich ass parents too. That had to be something Antoine could appreciate. Or would he? He heard the pages stop turning.

Now, she was staring at him.

"What?"

"You miss 'em, huh?"

A bitter snort escaped him before he could stop it. "You always into your client's business?"

"You ain't exactly hiding it there, guy." She quietly went back to flipping through the pages. "How long's it been?"

"Three weeks," he answered, his voice barely a whisper.

"Oh shit, man. That's raw."

"They buried…." He stopped himself with another painful wince. "The funeral was yesterday."

The tattooist's face was completely still. Not a trace of fake sympathy. "You weren't there, huh?"

He couldn't answer.

Instead of pressing him, she turned the book around again. "Okay, so this one here's for Papa Legba. He's more about life than death. Attuned to nature and all, so you got your cross-strokes there with the two leaves. It's smaller. I think it'd look good as a stomach piece, but that's totally your call."

Kyle gripped the counter with his fingers, the scrape of wood under his nails doing nothing to quell his anger or stop the tears that threatened to break down his face. He'd been at the funeral all right. He'd come ready with some bullshit story about knowing Antoine from school, but he needn't have bothered. Not the way he'd been dressed. No member of the esteemed Lavolier family had wanted to talk to him, least of all Antoine's mom, who'd kept eyeballing him like a piece of white trash, which was exactly the way he'd felt for the hour or so they'd stood out there. How he still felt.

Now he was out getting a tattoo? His memorial to Antoine was a goddamn tattoo?

"I'm sorry," he said. "This was a bad idea."

"You changed your mind?"

"No. I mean... I just need..." He swallowed, silently clenching and releasing his fists. Go, he told himself. Just walk out of there and stop wasting this chick's time. Nobody wanted a dance from him because they could see his grief. A good dancer was a smiling, eager to please jock, ready to drop their shorts and party any time, any place. That was the fantasy. His job. Nobody wanted a mopey bitch in their lap.

"Did he know how much you cared about him?"

Kyle looked up at her, feeling the white heat of anger flash behind his eyes. "Who told you it was a him?"

"You. Just now. But I'd figured."

He nodded, his mouth tightening. He was a fucking mess. Might as well tattoo 'big fucking mess' on his forehead and get it over with. "Sorry for wasting your time," he said through gritted teeth before heading for the door.

"Hey," the woman called, flipping through the book once more. "Hold up. Let me show you something."

He peered at the page she turned toward him. On it was another, simpler veve, this one a crucifix with smaller crosses at each end, an intricate circle around its cross point, and two long bones crossing right above the low wall of bricks that formed its base.

"I've never actually done this one," the woman explained. "But if you want something a little different? Maybe a bit more...interesting?"

He looked closer, tracing the delicate lines with his finger. Compared to the other veves, it seemed so modest. Yet it piqued his curiosity. "Shoot," he murmured.

The artist grinned.

*   *   *

Kyle watched the last group of tourists leave the museum, then checked the time on his phone. Almost six. Just enough time to get in and satisfy his curiosity. The tourists seemed satisfied enough, leaving the museum with big smiles on their faces, clutching tiny bags probably full of books and knick-knacks, waving hands and pointing fingers, teasing each other with fake curses.

He touched the spot on his chest where the woman had inked him. Why the hell was he doing this?

The store that fronted the museum was a little plainer than he'd expected. No explosion of colorful tourist trinkets lined the walls. No cheesy dolls stuck with pins. No ominous signs cast in skeletal font forbidding photos. Just a few African masks on the walls, a couple of grinning skulls decorated with coins, beads, and the occasional knife, aged wooden boxes stocked with tiny colored bags, candles of every shape and color, figurines of the Virgin Mary, alongside other saints he didn't recognize, plus feathered figures of the Voodoo spirits he took to be the various loa the tattoo artist had described to him, some obviously more pitched at tourists than others.

But more than anything else, there were books. Books on spells and rituals, famous practitioners, the spirits... Kyle pulled one from the shelf, flipping directly to the index and holding it open with his thumb. He flipped through to the first of the five or six pages that mentioned Ghede Nibo, patron spirit of those taken before their time. Those whose deaths had defied justice, or were the product of violence. Deaths like—

"Closing in five, son. If you plan on dog-earing that volume any more, you'd best plan on buying it."

He peered at the old man gingerly stubbing a cigarette out in an ornate silver tray on the counter. Behind him, Kyle saw a small altar next to the doorway that led to the museum's entrance, a dim red light just visible behind its black curtain. "Yeah, umm...maybe."

"'May-be,' he says. May-be," the old guy mused, his accent carrying the pure, faintly aristocratic lilt of an educated man who, for all his worldliness, had known no other home but New Orleans. There was no trace of the southern drawl that gave away the guys at Laveau's as transplants, nor the faint Cajun affect that tinged Kyle's own words. Maybe he'd lucked out. Maybe this place, and this guy, were the genuine article.

"Hey, umm...you know anything about this Ghede Nibo?"

The guy nodded, slowly, pushing the ash tray aside. "I know enough about a lot of things. That includes the psychopomp."

"The what?" The word sounded like something you'd call a rave at a mad house.

"The psychopomp. An intermediary between the living and the dead. What's your interest in any case?"

Kyle shrugged, carefully putting the book back where he found it before pulling up his shirt and showing the man his still glistening tattoo.

The guy just stared at him, keen grey eyes dull and immutable, until he finally spoke. "So, which is it? Are you desperate or just plain stupid?"

He opened his mouth to speak but choked. What the hell was that supposed to mean? Hell, with his white hair and six chins sticking out under his ruddy pink face, the old guy looked more like he should be asking snot-nosed brats at the mall what they wanted for Christmas than cracking wise at customers in a Voodoo store.

"A messenger from the land of the unjustly dead, most of them fair rightly pissed off, I dare say, and you get his damn post-box tattooed over your heart? Sounds like a real wise idea, son. So, which is it? You desperate or just plain stupid?"

"I…I don't know. It's just ink."

"'Just ink,' he says. 'Just ink.' Probably the most dangerous substance on this here earth. There've been wars started by 'just ink.' But don't you worry, son. Hell, if you're looking to get a few extra dollars stuffed down your jock, you probably couldn't have picked a better spirit to blaspheme."

"Jesus, man. What the hell's wrong with you? You think you're scaring me with that hoodoo bullshit? Hey, you know what? Forget it. I'm good. Sorry if I wasted your precious time."

The man didn't so much as flinch at his sarcasm. If he was offended or scared behind those keen eyes, Kyle wasn't seeing it. The guy lit another cigarette, holding it in that faggy way between his index and middle fingers, letting the smoke gently swirl to the ceiling. The man took one long drag and ashed the tip. "Hoodoo," he finally said, his tone now bone dry, "is not what we teach here, son. It's another thing altogether. Folk magic."

"Okay." He nodded, trying to cool his tone. "Okay, fine. It's folk magic. Hoodoo is folk magic, and Voodoo is…somethin' else. I get it. All part of the same, ain't it?"

"Ahah, sure!" the man drawled, smiling through a transparent mockery of Kyle's own accent. Why don't you stick around a half hour? We'll be drinkin' snake blood from a 'gator's head and askin' my dear old Aunt Doris, dead fifteen years this September, how it goes. You know what? You're right. Get lost, son. You're starting to bother me."

"Hey! Will you just…?"

The man took another long drag off his cigarette. "Just what?"

"This Ghede Nibo guy. The psychopomp. You said he was like, an intermediary? That was your word. So if you contact him…what? You can talk to dead folk?"

The man scoffed. "Well, Jesus, son. Any half decent séance will let you do that, if the dead want to do talking. Truth is, if they're happy, they do not give one damn about you or me or any other soul still living, breathing, eating, or worrying on this earth. Now, if they've got a bone to pick, a grudge against this earth, or their time on it, or *someone* on it, that would be a different story."

"You mean if they're like, murdered or something?"

"Hell, son. Murdered, accidental… Lots of ways to go before your time. Or just die unhappy or in pain. But you see, that's where there might be an anchor, to somebody left behind. And if old Ghede accepts your offering? He can make an unhappy soul feel a little less unloved."

The room felt hot all of a sudden. Kyle could feel the sweat forming on his brow, the clammy dampness of his palms. "What if he doesn't accept it?"

"The psychopomp's not that choosy, boy. You'll always have something he wants. Have no fear of that. Especially now you've seen fit to paint his veve under your tit." The old man slowly rose from his chair with a series of discordant creaks, taking a shiny black walking stick from behind it, then staggering toward the door. "So who'd you lose, if I'm not prying?"

"Huh? No…nobody. Just wanted to know more about my tat, is all."

The man turned over the sign in the storefront window, locking the door firmly beneath it before turning back to him. "Son, I hope for your sake that you're a better dancer than you are a liar."

"Hey, how'd you know I dance?"

The man shot him a dejected look. "New Orleans born and raised, dear boy. I'm acquainted with the type." The guy stepped closer, but he didn't press Kyle for an answer to his earlier question. "I'm leaving here in ten minutes. You've got 'til then. Second room on the left, if you don't want to waste time."

Kyle swallowed, silently nodding his thanks as he turned toward the black curtain.

"Hey!" The old guy stopped him. "Six fifty. We've all got a jock to stuff here, kid."

Kyle tried to force the image as far from mind as possible, fishing what singles he could from his shorts and dumping them on the desk.

Satisfied, the man tilted his head at the black curtain, lifting another cigarette to his lips.

*   *   *

If the gift shop had been a neat, well-ordered array of tourist-friendly books, knick-knacks and colorful charms, the three rooms behind the curtain were the playground of a full-blown, Voodoo-fevered imagination. A half dozen skeletons wore ragged furs and garish pimp hats. Skulls, crucifixes, and charms Kyle didn't recognize were hung up on walls, while peacock feathers added just a splash of extra color to the decor. Wooden masks on the shelf grinned at him with grim, mirthless smiles. Carved figures with melted candles and offering-filled bowls sat on tables covered with ornate red, brown, and pink cloths. Portraits of saints covered the walls, interspersed with aged papers attempting to explain hoodoo, the art of speaking to the dead and zombiism.

Shit. Ten minutes, the man had said. Probably five by now.

Kyle made for the room to which the old man had directed him. Second on the left, where he could hear faint music crackling on an old-style gramophone. Hard to get lost in a place this small. At least physically.

Great, he sniffed to himself. Now the old guy almost had him taking this shit half seriously.

A huge tapestry hung on the back wall of the room. At its center sat a woman he took to be the Virgin Mary. She looked the type anyway. Weren't they all the same in some way? Having been raised, scolded, and rejected by Baptists, Kyle had no way to know. Catholics, Buddhists, Mooslims, Hindoos were all the disciples of Satan in the expert eye of Reverend Charles McAlistair. At least until McAlistair had been caught with his dick inside a Mexican hustler named Pablo. Saint Pablo, as a fifteen-year-old Kyle had called him to the two or three friends who would listen and laugh at his jokes. But if the Reverend McAlistair's sins had bound him for hell, then by his own logic, he'd meet every Catholic, Buddhist, Mooslim, Hindoo, and no doubt Voodoo he'd decried in the quest to do 'God's holy work.'

This tapestry would have made McAlistair flip his shit. On either side of the Virgin, sat or stood a row of black faces painted with either white death's heads a touch larger than life, or just purple lipstick and eye shadow. A banquet of fruit, peppers, and the odd dead chicken, still unplucked, was spread on the table in front of them. A weird-ass picture, even by Voodoo standards, Kyle guessed, not that he had any idea what those standards would be. He couldn't decide if it was sacred, or a sacrilegious mockery of an old, famous painting of Jesus he thought he remembered, put up to please or shock visitors.

He cast his eye down the figures. He recognized Baron Samedi, the grinning poster child whenever somebody needed Voodoo to look flashy enough to spook the crowds. An old man sat at the end of the table, dressed in only a long red brown loincloth, a stick laying on the ground by his side, watched over by a shaggy brown dog. Legba, of course. At least the miniscule amount Kyle had learned about Voodoo in the past week wasn't letting him down completely.

He turned his attention away from the touristy centerpiece, letting the repetitive drone of the record wash over him. The melancholic gospel lilt was so strong he could barely make out the words. He cast his gaze down the smaller paintings and plaques that interpreted the spirits. Baron Samedi. His wife, Maman Brigitte. Kyle had started French in junior high with the best intentions, along with a half dozen or so others in his class. One by one, they'd dropped out, cursing the name of the teacher who'd told him plain as dirt that his accent *rendue malade*. No fewer than ten loa had earned a spot on the museum's wall. But save Samedi, Brigitte, and Papa Legba, they all seemed to read the same, at least to Kyle. Intermediary between our world and the spirits. Guardian of the dead. Likes offerings of cigars, hot peppers, chickens, or sugar. Tied to the Catholic saint of, blah, blah, blah, blah… Sure, the guy at the front counter could probably set him straight on most of them, but going another round with the cantankerous old fart was the last thing Kyle felt like doing. Besides, he'd thrown down his six fifty and still not found nothing useful. Nothing about the so-called 'psychopomp' the man had felt warranted such a warning.

The eleventh portrait was tucked away in the shadow of a human mannequin, which had been topped off with a stuffed alligator's head, a small top hat completing the look. Pure class, Kyle sniffed. He peered past the leathery green snout, squinting at the words. Nibo. Another 'guardian of the dead.' But what the fuck was he looking at?

The figure in the portrait stood with its hips cocked in a pose so sissified, even the drags at Oz would have cringed. Around those dark hips were a pair of lacy pink girl's underwear, which topped what seemed to Kyle—he couldn't really tell with the poster in shadow—to be a long pair of black stocking-clad legs, which stretched down into knee-high purple boots. The boots were the same purple as the long coat that hung from the figure's shoulders. As Kyle peered closer, looking at the figure's face, the one feature he could see clearly in the dim light, he saw the eyelids and lips had been painted the same garish shade. From between those lips, the thing grinned at him in a way he didn't like one bit.

He cast his eye down to the description. Ghede Nibo. An intermediary between the living and the dead, and the patron of those lost before their time. Those who were murdered, or who'd died in horrible accidents. Even the circumstances surrounding Nibo's own death were open to interpretation, though most agreed he'd died young, only to be adopted in the spirit world by Samedi and Brigitte, from whom he'd inherited a foul mouth, a taste for the familiar offerings of the Voodoo faithful, and a trickster's sense of humor.

A sense of humor? A sense of fucking humor? The supposed patron saint of young murder victims was laughing about it? Kyle looked again at the portrait. At the boots, the stockings, the panties, the lurid grin. Grotesque.

Antoine would never have worn that shit. Sure, Antoine would put on lipstick, maybe some bling like dangling earrings or a bracelet. A girl's belt cinching trim pants around his waist. Or maybe a girl's jacket. But when Antoine wore it, he was his own man, carrying himself so confidently it didn't matter what anybody thought. Six foot two of skinny black boy, whose mere presence let you know he wasn't to be fucked with. And whose voice…

Kyle knew Antoine had sensed something different in his stare, different to the stares from the rest of the bar. Different enough to draw Antoine in, his fingers like velvet as they slipped over the flesh of Kyle's arm. That first touch was what Kyle remembered most. The first time he'd felt Antoine's skin against his, sitting there with two stupid grins on their lipstick-smeared faces.

He also remembered the laughter. Not the laughs he'd shared with Antoine, but the laughter of the people around them. Most of it had been quiet, leaking from behind colorful drinks or cocky sneers. But the eyes had been the tell on every last one of them. Everyone enjoying the same joke. The dumb white hick, his face smeared from kissing the silly, pretty black faggot. He'd felt their stares. Maybe even their pity. But at the time, none of it had mattered. Each time they'd started up, either Kyle or Antoine, sometimes the both of them together, would draw closer, shutting the world around them out behind the sweetness of another kiss.

He looked again at the ridiculous grin and distinctly sexual tilt of the spirit's bearing. That was it. The fear Antoine had taken away. The fear that that's what strangers saw, even in a gay bar. In Antoine. Maybe even in him. It was definitely what his father and uncle saw.

Then, he noticed it. In the top right-hand corner of the description, that fucking 'veve.' The design he'd had stuck under his skin. A permanent symbol of this grinning faggot. Protector of the dead? What kind of bullshit was that? That so-called protector was laughing at him now. Just like they all had.

He turned away, facing a small altar draped in red, gold, and brown cloth. A statue of a saint he didn't recognize sat in its center, flanked on either side by low burning candles. Small bowls of orange and brown powders sat in front of the statue. They could have been pepper, cinnamon, or fucking dirt for all he knew. A trio of bare stems lay spread around the bowl, surrounded by the colorful petals he guessed had been scraped off them, probably by the small, ornate knife on the altar. On the wall beside it was another portrait, so old and dark he could barely make out the figure at its center. Probably some other so-called god or hoodoo witch who watched over the graveyard or whatever. Or maybe the old guy out front had a crazy aunt who owned half of this shit and put her own portrait up for shits and giggles. He didn't care anymore. The clearest image in the frame was his own, reflected back at him in the dusty glass.

Even in the dim reflection, he could see the dark circles around his eyes. When had he last slept? Really slept through the night proper? He couldn't remember. Sleepless. Stupid. Now he was getting fucking Voodoo spirits tattooed on him without even knowing what they meant?

"Two minutes, son."

He barely heard the old man's voice from the front as he took hold of his shirt and pulled it up over his head. The reflection of the tattoo was clear. Dark, crisp, and new against his pasty skin. The spirit's mailbox, so the old man had said. The leering faggot's mark.

He hated it. He hated the spirit. He hated himself. He hated the damned symbol.

He snatched up the knife and felt it pierce his chest before he could think twice. He then gritted his teeth, forcing down the scream. Just what the hell had he planned to do? Was he nuts? He couldn't just cut it out. They had lasers and shit for that stuff now, not that he could ever afford that. But it was too late. The first cut had gone deep. It bled all over his fingers as he tried to stem it. Shit!

He looked around for a cloth, a handkerchief, or anything else he could use to wipe his hand and if he was lucky, cover his ruined tat until it finished bleeding. Fuck! Stupid shithead! What the hell had made him think he could grab a knife and do that shit himself?

"Son?"

"I'll just be a minute!" he yelled back, wiping his hands on a red cloth covering the altar. He cursed, seeing the vivid, ugly streaks of blood, then cleaned the rest on the purple cloth. Better. He could still see it, but it didn't seem as harsh and dirty as it did on the red. He picked up the knife again and cleaned it on the same cloth. But there was too much blood. Far more than he'd expected. Damn. Did he need a hospital? He couldn't afford that shit either.

He looked around for something to wipe the blood on, jolting as he caught a glimpse of the portrait. Ghede Nibo was every bit as obscene as it had seemed in the other picture, blown up to a size that filled the frame, leering down at him. Kyle backed away, tripped on a fold in the rug and fall hard on his ass, crying out as he cut himself again with the knife. The old gramophone continued its steady droning, the gentle hiss of vinyl under the needle as the spirit faded from the picture frame, leaving only the darkness of the indistinct figure he'd seen before. The words of the song seemed clearer now, as Kyle tried to steady himself, if only to stop his stomach churning.

Time for judgment. Time for pain. If the good Lord will give a righteous man his...

Kyle jumped as someone hammered at the door to the small room. He couldn't remember closing it, and it sure hadn't slammed shut.

"I don't find this at all amusing, son. You hear?"

Oh Lord, take this wretched fool away.

"Be...be right there," he stammered. "Sorry."

"Goddamn it."

Let him be restored anew. Restored anew...

Kyle would have given anything to rip the record off the gramophone and smash it on the altar. But the old guy was probably pissed enough with him already. He winced as he brought the cloth up to his bleeding chest. It burned like... Fuck! That wasn't normal, was it? Was there ground pepper or something on the cloth?

Let him be your righteous hand...

He glanced up at the portrait again, sure he could see the grinning faggot once more. He couldn't be sure. The light on the portrait seemed to flicker on and off. But that was impossible because... Fuck! He turned to face the door, then he kept on turning. Or maybe it was the room, turning around him, another nasty hoodoo trick on his senses. Maybe from something on the cloth he used to stem the bleeding. Maybe from the weird smelling candles on the altar. He couldn't be sure. The room seemed to spin over and over and over, until he steadied himself on the altar, sending the two bowls of powder skittering off the surface and onto the floor with two sharp thuds.

The wound started burning again. He'd thrown away the cloth, but his tattoo still itched like crazy. The song on the record had stopped, leaving the soft hiss of needle on vinyl as the only sound in the room. Even the hammering on the door had fallen silent.

The portrait seemed even darker when he looked at it again, staring mostly into his own reflection, his eye drawn to the blood that still trickled down his chest. Could he get it fixed? Would it heal on its own? He touched it gingerly, wincing as it stung.

"What wounds your heart, little boy?"

The voice had been soft and high, like the rustling of a snake in long grass, the record player crackling quietly beneath it. Kyle shivered as a sudden chill broke over his naked shoulders. He brought his bloodstained fingers up to his face, staring into the red drop at the end of them.

"There is no shame in pain, little cocksucker," the voice purred again. "What would soothe a broken soul?"

Kyle shook his head, wiping the spot of blood on his pants. "All right, I'll go!" he yelled at the old man he guessed was still outside. "Real fucking funny, man. Real cute." His shoe caught in the rug before he could take a single step, sending him sprawling onto his stomach. He groaned, hoping nothing was broken as he lifted his gaze to the door, then looked back over his shoulder.

"There is no shame in blood."

The voice was coming from the record. He didn't understand how. He didn't try. It was all he could do to lay there, barely breathing until it stopped. If it stopped.

"He bleeds for you, too. He cries for you."

Kyle swallowed, awkwardly flipping onto his back as the voice continued. What was it? How did it know anything about him? About Antoine? "What…" How could he know what to ask? Especially if the thing already knew so damn much.

"What do you seek here, little boy?" the voice purred. "You wish to be with him again?"

His gaze fell on the knife once more. He'd sure as hell thought about it. Ending it quickly. Antoine had been the only one who'd accepted him. Shown him any kind of respect. Maybe even love. He slowly lifted up the knife, wincing as its cold blade touched his throat. Come on, chickenshit! Make it quick.

A slow, high-pitched laugh mocked him from the record player. "Oh, that's a plan, little cocksucker. You think you will find him on the plain of the dead? There are millions on that plain. Millions hurting, like him. Like you."

Kyle tightened his grip on the blade hilt, lowering it. He briefly considered throwing it at the damn portrait. Or the record player. Or just at the wall, somewhere. He had to be imagining this. Some weird hoodoo shit had to be fucking with his brain. He'd been less than an inch from offing himself, probably in the most painful way he could imagine. Quick? Like hell. He'd probably even fuck that up. The result would be anything but quick.

"What else do you want, little boy? Forgiveness, that you could not help him? Justice?"

The word fired through him like an electric charge. He hadn't much thought about that. If the cops hadn't caught the bastard, what hope did he have? But had they really tried? Some black faggot wearing heels and makeup shows up dead near the Quarter? Hell, Antoine's parents didn't even want the story out there.

"You feel it, little boy. Do not lie to me."

"Yes," he whispered. "Yeah...yeah I—"

"Yeeeeeeees," the voice hissed, its voice rising into strange, mewling laughter. "Old Ghede can give you what you want."

Kyle shivered. He'd known who it was, of course. He'd known it the moment he'd accepted he wasn't going crazy.

"You...you can bring Antoi—"

"What you ask is no small favor. If a lost soul is to be found, then one must take its place."

Kyle swallowed, staring at the knife's blade once more, touching his fingers to his throat.

"No, little boy. Why should your own blood pay for an evil man's sins? Love for love. Blood for blood. Old Ghede can bring this evil man to you."

"You...you can do that? For me?"

"It will take time, little one. This man knows your face. Knows your lust."

Kyle's grip tightened around the knife, so hard it almost hurt. No. It couldn't be. No fucking way!

"A daemon with the face of angels," the spirit purred. "How did it feel, to grip the cock of the man who would be your lover's murd—"

"*Fuck you!*"

The record hissed, faint cracks popping every few seconds as he listened, barely breathing.

"You must approach him with a face he does not know, little boy," the thing said, finally breaking its silence. "And play the part for as long as you will, to gain his trust."

"A face he doesn't know?" Kyle spat back. "And just how the hell am I supposed to do that? Hell, I don't need this shit. I'll follow that bastard home right after he's done dancin'."

"Oooooh, clever plan, little boy. To murder a man so close to you? Try using whatever stuffs that pretty faggot head of yours! The secret of your crime wouldn't last a day."

The thing had a point. What had he been thinking? Follow the son of a bitch home and then what? Go back to the bar where everyone knew who he was and how much he hated that bastard?

"I...I want to do it myself. I've got to, damn it!"

"Don't worry, little cocksucker. Ghede will hide your beautiful face until the deed is done. And he will hide your memories, lest they betray you."

He noticed the light growing brighter on the portrait. A stranger stared back at him from behind the glass. A stranger with short cropped hair, its deep, dark brown dotted with tiny flecks of grey. The jaw seemed harder, a little squarer than his own, while a distinctly harder nose cut the line between two plain brown eyes. Handsome. Hell, it reminded him of one of the guys he remembered from his uncle's farm. He frowned, and the image frowned back.

Shit.

He touched a hand to the glass, only to have the figure return the gesture in kind, staring back at him with those mournful, brown eyes. They might have been a different color, but they held all of his uncertainty. All of his fears, sadness, and hate. *Hide your beautiful face until the deed is done?*

Oh, shit.

Hell, if the spirit was offering him this chance, he'd be stupid not to take it. He gripped the knife again, liking the sound of this deal more and more. If the spirit led Antoine's murderer to him, he'd kill the bastard then and there. And if the guy had friends, or if any son-of-a-bitch got in his way...

"Ghede knows your heart, little cocksucker. Best to arrest your bloodlust. Ghede cares not for it. Abusing his offering, violating his law has consequences. Blood for blood. Love for love. No more. No less."

Kyle swallowed, still unable to quell the anger that gripped his throat. Could the thing read his thoughts? Because he'd meant every one of them. "What do you mean by that? What if this guy had friends? Hell, maybe he didn't do this by himself!"

"Is it so hard, little boy?" the thing snarled. "This man's life for the life of your love. No more, no less. Any other is not your prey. Of this, I warn you above all. Do not compound his crime with sins of your own, lest you become the very monster you seek."

"I..." Kyle choked, looking at the knife as he turned it over in his hand. "I get it, but what if..."

"Swear to me that you will honor Ghede's law, little one," the voice snapped, now possessing a rough, jagged edge. "Else he wastes no more time on you."

He felt the weight of the knife in his hand. Blood for blood. "All right. All right, I swear, damn it. Now what? I'm s'posed to cut my hand or something?"

An unseen force gripped his wrist, bringing the knife back up to his chest and cutting a deep gash into it. He screamed, trying to free his fingers, but the knife continued its vicious dance over his skin, cutting each line of his tattoo's intricate design until it was a mess of red gashes, streaming blood muddled with ink and tears down his chest. When the blade at last slipped from his fingers, he stared, slack-jawed at the dark image staring down at him, finally collapsing to the floor. It took every scrap of energy he had to breathe. Just breathe. In, out, in, out. Ignore the searing pain in his chest or the ebbing blood now running away into the old man's rug.

"Son?" a voice called as the door started rattling again. "Goddamn it, boy. Open this door or I'm calling the police."

He silently mewled an indistinct response before the room went dark.

MARC

The heat and humidity had spread across the city like some fat-assed tourist across a tiny bar stool. They saw the type every day this time of year. Former frat boys grown old, but not grown up, hiding from the sun in stinking bars on Bourbon, too wasted to realize it was noon.

Staying inside was probably the one smart decision still within reach of their Hurricane-soaked brains, but it had driven Marc and Ash's chances of a decent take down to almost zero. The crowds were thinner. Fewer and fewer johns were coming to the bar, and Marc lacked the pickpocketing skills some other guys used to pick up the slack. He also had no great desire to use them. He had no problem stripping or dancing. Even hustling. The johns got their money's worth, and he got paid. It was all good. But he wasn't a thief. He'd snatched a guy's wallet right out of his hand on the riverfront once, before losing the guy in a crowd watching a second line on Decatur. His one attempt had been a success, but it had felt alien, like it was beneath him. It hadn't impressed Ash either.

"Eighty bucks? You want cops on your ass for eighty lousy bucks?"

And Ash was right. It'd be the last time. Maybe the heat had sent him a little crazy, like it sometimes did to Ash.

This time, Ash had gone fucking mental.

It had taken just one night, after Dan had lifted the ban Marc's performance had earned them from the bar. Marc had tried to play by the rules. No fancy flesh-work or stray hard-ons, no matter how much the johns whooped and hollered for a repeat performance. They remembered him, all right. "Fire hose in the house," one of them had called out, to the loud amusement of several others.

Sure enough, while Marc had been gratefully tucking away his singles and fives, Ash had picked up some European john in town for Decadence. One who was more than willing to take the local talent back to the apartment he'd rented somewhere off Esplanade. At least, that was where he'd led them. The guy's accent hadn't much helped communication. Had he also misunderstood them? Or had Ash been his usual, slippery-ass self about their oh-so-negotiable terms? It didn't much matter. Not now that the man was on the ground, bleeding, cowering to protect himself.

"What do you mean 'no money'?" Ash screamed.

When the guy didn't answer, Ash kicked him again.

"Stop! I not know you were—"

"Ash, calm the fuck down, man!" Marc said.

This was bad. What if the guy went to the cops? Fuck, he surely would. And the cops knew Dan, and Dan knew their faces and phone numbers. The names they tricked under. Hell, half the queers in the Quarter could probably recognize them.

"Didn't know I was what?" Ash's anger simmered as he caught his breath.

"Ash, come on man. Leave him. We've got his face. If he starts any shit, we'll find him." Marc only wished he could feel as brave as his words as he hissed at their victim. "You hear that? You say nothing, nothing to anyone. Not the cops, not the fucking hospital. You got yourself wasted and got in a fight on your way home. You got that?"

It was the truth, technically. The guy just glowered, his face still bleeding from where Ash had pummeled him down.

"Do you understand?"

"Marc," Ash interrupted, his voice low. "Come on, Eurotrash. Didn't know I was what?"

The man's busted lip curled up into a snarl, his hand balled into a fist. "Stupid fucking Americans!"

"What the fuck are you—?"

"You think I pay for you, dumb ass? You want money? In Holland, you fucking say so. But here." The Dutchman jerkily clawed a slim wallet out of his jeans and threw it at them. It was nearly empty. Of course it fucking was. Any cash he'd had at the start of the night had already been tucked into Marc's jock. Or Ash's. Or...hell, they were damn fools, all three of them. "Take all the money you want. Stupid, dumb faggot whore."

"Ash!"

It was too late. Ash had already slammed his boot into the guy's stomach. The next one crashed through his teeth, sending one flying into the darkness. With that, the Dutch guy was perfectly still. Trickles of blood flowed steadily from where his head lay.

"Ash," Marc said. "He's not moving."

"Shut the fuck up." Ash started to kick the man again and again, sending his boot into the still body with a steady thud. "Get up. Come on, get up you bastard. Call me a—"

"Ash" Marc's wide-eyed gaze darted around the darkened houses. "We gotta go."

"He...is...no, he's not. Get up, you faggot cunt!" Ash screamed at the man's still, breathless body.

Marc grabbed Ash's arm and ran, not stopping or even slowing down until they'd left the lights, tourists, and cops of the Quarter far behind. They passed through the lights and music of Frenchman Street, heading deep into the warehouses behind the Marigny, far from where anyone would find the body of a dead Dutch tourist. No, he wouldn't think like that. Someone would find the guy and help him out. Somebody had to. Shit!

Ash broke from his grip and rested his hands on his knees, catching his breath. There was blood on his boot.

"What'd you do?" Marc asked. "Fuck! What is wrong with you, man? Why'd you—"

"What? You heard that prick. Call me a—"

Marc was on Ash like a daemon, grabbing his shoulders and shoving him against the wall. "That's not a goddamn reason!" he screamed. "He's gone Ash! You fucking kil—"

Ash's hand shot up and grabbed Marc's throat before he could stop it. There were no words. Just those cold, blue eyes that, in that moment, didn't know him. Didn't care one bit about him.

Marc choked as Ash released him, stumbling as he regained his feet and breath.

"You heard him," Ash hissed, seething. "You think he's right? You think I'm a faggot?"

"Ash—"

"Do you?"

"You shake your ass for them and suck their dicks for money!" Marc flinched as Ash grabbed him again, by his shoulders this time. The strength in those hands terrified him, and yet feeling it pinned against his arms felt...steady, somehow. Ash's hands were strong, powerful and unchanging. Marc felt his breath slow as he relaxed into their grip. If Ash had meant to beat him, he'd be on the ground already.

Fuck! They'd...yeah, *they*, together, had just killed a man. A man who'd be found first thing come morning. A man who'd been seen, hell, probably caught on tape leaving the bar with Ash. And Marc had been a part of it. He could dress it up any way he wanted, but he'd done nothing to help. He'd just stood back, tossing out useless words while Ash had beaten the life out of the guy.

"We..." Marc stammered. "We need to get that guy an ambulance. We could go to a bar on Frenchman. Somewhere crowded. You distract some drunk dude, while I get his phone. The guy gets help... Hell, he's not gonna say nothing. We scared the shit out of him. What do you say?"

Ash's face hadn't changed. "Is he right?" he asked quietly. "Am I a faggot, Marc?"

Marc could only swallow.

"Fine. You show me."

He gasped as Ash shoved him down onto his knees. "Show me what a faggot you think I am."

Marc's stomach turned over as his gaze rose from the blood on Ash's boots to the swollen erection that now filled Ash's jeans. He must have shaken his head, since the next thing he felt was Ash's hand across his face.

"Jesus, Ash," he whimpered, nursing his cheek. "Not now."

"Show me what a faggot I am, you little bitch."

His hands shaking, Marc slowly rolled open Ash's fly and freed his cock, wrapping his lips around it before he could decide if Ash actually was a faggot or if his hard-on was from the gruesome rush of killing the Dutch guy.

"I can't," he choked, trying to spit it out.

Ash pushed his cock deeper into Marc's lips. Marc tried not to think about his own manhood as it started to swell. It didn't matter if Ash was a fag or bisexual or into him or just winding him up or using him or whatever the fuck he was doing. The guy's body, his scent, the weight and taste of his cock, the salt of his precum, and the unmatched feeling of it all pushing hard into him, turned Marc on for real. He thought about it all, about how Ash's touch had made him shiver, sent that welcome coolness right through him, cutting right through the humidity of the summer night.

He hated all of it now.

He tried to focus on Ash's cock. Cold and uninvolved, like he was just another john, but it was no use. Ash was moaning the way he always did when he wanted Marc to know he was pleasing him. But while Marc knew it was a gross mockery of appreciation, the smooth, satisfied voice was too familiar to ignore. The skull above the guy's groin mocked him too, grinning at Marc from under the thin cloth of Ash's tank top. It taunted him. Marc remembered how he'd kissed that skull. How he'd tried to be so soft and gentle, stroking the blonde hairs of Ash's leg as he'd flicked his tongue over his navel.

He hated everything that had ever drawn him to Ash.

Marc grabbed a fistful of Ash's tank and yanked it up. He closed his eyes, focused on keeping up his steady rhythm around Ash's cock. Instead, it was like fireworks going off beneath his eyelids. Sudden, bright flashes of greens, reds, and blues fired across the darkness he'd hoped would relax him. It hurt too much to keep his eyes shut, just as Ash was hurting the back of his throat, pushing his cock as deep as it would go.

Harder. Faster. Smoother. Anything to get it over with soon.

He was already on the verge of choking when he opened his eyes to see the face staring back at him from Ash's stomach. It was no longer a skull, but the grinning, dark visage of a handsome young man. One whose mascara accentuated long black lashes, and whose lips popped a shade of purple as seductive as it was sickening. Against logic or reason, Marc knew it. He knew its name. Felt it so close to the tip of his tongue. He tried to spit out Ash's cock again, but the shaft refused to budge from inside his throat. Like the spirit had pinned it there for its own cruel amusement.

"Oh, fearful child," the face purred in a voice neither fearsome nor loving. It wasn't even remotely human. It sounded like the last high pitched, nasal breaths of a man getting sucked down into a swamp. A low growl that broke over the hiss of snakes.

Marc closed his eyes again, trying to will the image away.

"Look at me when I talk to you, cocksucker!"

A sudden wind chilled Marc's shoulders. Ash tasted different. Wrong somehow, like...

He jumped with a start, looking up to see the wicked face of the spirit grinning down at him where Ash had been not a moment before, its great cock wedged firmly inside his mouth. The smooth planes of its body were laid bare between the lapels of a long pink coat, under which it wore matching lace panties, tucked under two swollen, dark balls. And at the base of its stomach...

Marc tried to push away, tried to free himself from the creature, whose appendage now held him by the throat. With one final hard push against its body, he freed himself, but he could still feel the swollen presence against his throat, filling his mouth as he grasped at the air with futility. Marc felt the cold, reptilian scales slide under his fingers as he finally latched onto it. Its head whipped around to face him, but instead of a serpent's eyes and flicking tongue, he found himself eye to eye with the grinning head of the strange being, its dark features vivid with eye shadow, lipstick, and rouge. Marc tried to speak, but the snake's tail was too far swollen inside his throat to allow him to form words.

"What is this?" the face asked. The voice was the same, except now it had taken on the exaggerated Caribbean tones of one of the con men who screwed tourists into getting their bones read or whatever. "Did you forget me, fucking ungrateful faggot? That's no good. That's no fucking good at all." The last word became a high nasal wail as the serpent thing's head tilted back to fix Ash with its upside-down gaze.

Marc tore his eyes away. Off to his right, he saw a drawn and shriveled body, pale and utterly still. Ash? It couldn't be. The body's fingers were marked by a sickening tinge of blue at the tips, and what was left of its lips seemed purple to the point of blackness. It looked ghoulish against the blond hair faded almost white, and the now anemic look of its tattoos.

There was no mistaking it. Ash.

"Remember now, little faggot?" the creature's voice whined again, rising to face Marc. "Remember what I promised you?

This time, it wasn't the apparition's face but another, gently dark and so beautiful, with soft lips and dark, wide eyes. Almost comforting in its familiarity and yet so frightened.

"A...Ash?"

"Noooooo." The spirit's voice resumed its wailing pitch.

"Who... I don't—"

"DO YOU REMEMBER???"

Marc jumped back as the face lurched toward him, teeth bared, eyes wide, filled with righteous anger. Marc felt the soft flesh break between his teeth as he snapped his jaw shut in fright and tasted blood.

A great scream erupted with full force into the night. It was very, very human.

The black scales of the serpent god thing were no more. In their place, he saw only Ash's pasty white skin. His friend's face contorted with agony, frozen with the scream that had pierced the night and broken whatever spell had left Marc so deluded he'd seen snakes with the heads of ancient Voodoo spirits. No. Loa. That was the word. He remembered now.

Fuck! He could taste the blood on his lips. Ash was clutching himself where Marc's mouth had just been. His mind had picked a hell of a time to be dreaming up nightmares.

"You dumb redneck cunt!" Ash cracked a fist across Marc's jaw.

The world spun around Marc like he'd been drinking. He'd only just made out the white shape of Ash bearing down on him when another fist slammed into his gut. Then another. He felt Ash grab his shoulder.

"What's wrong with you, bitch?" Ash snarled, voice reaching a shrill, nerve jarring crescendo. "You fucking crazy now? Crazy ass faggot?"

"Ash, stop! I was..."

Even if he'd been able to right his thoughts, how did he explain this? He'd just bitten the cock of a man he'd watched murder a guy in a blazing rage. It was sure as fuck not something he could pin on Voodoo spirits and snakes.

"Ash! I can't—"

Another fist landed across his jaw, setting his head spinning again. A mad panic seized his insides, some fierce, protective instinct that made his chest burn beneath its scars.

"Fuck off!" Marc twisted free and shoved Ash sprawling to the ground. He drove a strong boot into Ash's wounded manhood, ignoring his scream as Marc ran in the direction of the Bywater, around another corner and over two chain fences. It wasn't long before he was lost. He could feel the blood running down his face. He wiped a trickle of it from his cheek, wincing as he touched a cut under his eye. Tears mingled with blood on the tips of his fingers. He should have felt more scared. He'd find his way back to the Quarter soon enough, if Ash didn't find him first and leave him behind a dumpster as dead as they'd left the Dutch guy. Had Ash actually killed him? Shit! Had it been the first time? There was something about that face. The one he'd seen replace the spirit on the end of the snake. Strange, yet familiar as hell.

"Bark!"

He turned to face the furry intruder. The scrawny mutt grinned at him in the dim light. He ignored it, too focused on catching his breath and getting out of there. Out of the Bywater and away from any place Ash would look for him. Maybe even home. Could he go back ho...

Where was home? Everything about it seemed hazy now. A few vague memories of a dirt road and boarded-up shop windows. Some place where you nodded with a fake smile at every white face you passed and hoped nobody knew you liked to suck dick. Would Mom and Dad even want to see him? Mom... Dad... He couldn't even picture their faces any more than he could picture the town or remember its name. Ash had hit him hard.

"Marc," a voice whispered in his head. "Marc!"

It came louder this time. The voice of his mother? His father? It was a man's voice all right, but not his Dad's.

"Bark!"

The dog's bark was friendly and familiar, full of love without judgment. The dog knew him. That made no sense either.

"Hey," he whispered, squatting to his haunches, slow and controlled as he stared into the mutt's eyes. What the hell? Couldn't hurt, could it? "Come here. Come here, boy."

The dog ran at him, tongue hanging stupidly out as he lapped it over Marc's cheeks over and over, like it was trying to wake him up. Its wet, sandpapery texture tickled. On any other night, he could have laughed.

"Hey, cut it out," he whispered, taking the dog in his arms.

Instantly, it fell deathly still. He stared into its now glassy eyes, like he could somehow catch the last strains of life before they drained out. It didn't seem real. He wasn't feeling anything. No sadness, just fascination. This wasn't his dog. He'd never owned a dog. That much he knew for sure.

The thing couldn't have just up and died, even if it had gone stiff as concrete in his arms. Sure enough, its head slowly rose, lopsided on its lifeless body. Again, its snout parted into a canine grin as it looked up at him.

"All is well, little cocksucker. You don't have to remember me."

Marc cried out as the animal snapped at him, dropping it onto the ground as its frozen limbs cricked back to life. One paw, then another, each inch of movement seeming a little less difficult and more fluid than the last. The beast's claws clicked along the concrete as it dragged itself forward, faster and faster, building momentum as it covered more ground.

"Marc!" Ash's voice. "Get back here, bitch! We ain't done!"

The dog shot off into the darkness.

Marc didn't even think. He took off after it, desperate to keep up. It may not have been his, but it had talked. It had spoken to him, goddamn it. And if he'd imagined it all, if all this shit had been cooked up inside his head, he wanted to know why. Even if the mutt wasn't his, something about it seemed familiar, like dozens of memories locked away just over his mind's horizon. Mom's face. Dad's. The town he grew up in. He'd felt them all as he'd clung to the creature. Just out of reach.

"Marc!"

He ignored Ash's rage, too focused on the dog to break his stride. It had squeezed through a hole in a rusty chain link gate. Marc eyed it, imagining the harsh, rusty wire scratching his skin. He was sure he could climb it, but it looked... Fuck it! He had bigger worries than goddamn tetanus.

The wire felt cold in the humid air as he climbed. One, two... over... ouch!

He dropped to the other side of the gate and steadied himself, staring at the blood seeping from the tear in his hand. He gently sucked on it.

Bark! Bark! Bark!

Marc started coughing. Great. Like the dog wasn't getting enough of Ash's attention. He ducked into a narrow street wedged behind the back of two rows of shotgun houses. A darkened warehouse loomed behind them. The rusty fence, the well-lit door with its bags of trash on either side of broken brick steps. The darkened door on the other side of the lane. He had no idea where the fuck he was. Through the cold sting of the rain, he could smell piss and blood. The scents of death.

The dog trotted off into the darkness until Marc could no longer distinguish between it and the building. He could only just make out a set of eyes, kind and dark, yet reddened by tears. As his vision adjusted, Marc began to make out the edges of a bum wrapped in soiled, dark clothing. Some part of him wished just a few of those tears were for him. He didn't know why. Hell, others deserved them more. Like the Dutch guy.

"You remember now, little boy?" the voice rumbled in the dark. "Your blood. His blood. Your soul. His soul. Can you smell it? The stain of his sin."

Marc froze as he heard the rattling of the gate, followed by the rubber thud of Ash's boots hitting the pavement. Marc swallowed as he heard the flick of Ash's knife. This was a place of death, all right. Maybe even his own.

Ash stared at him, eyes blazing. Still, past the anger and outrage, Marc saw something else in those eyes. Respect. Not the kind that was earned or deserved, but the kind spawned of raw shock. Ash had been running hard and his breath was heavy. The lights of the surrounding buildings shone behind his blond hair like a grotesque halo.

"What the hell is wrong with you, bitch?" Ash screamed. "What are you trying to do?"

Marc choked, staring down at the blade of Ash's knife. "I...I'm sorry. It was an accident."

"You accidentally bit my—"

"I freaked out, man. We just left that guy. He's probably dead."

"So?"

"So? I have a big fuckin' problem with that. You kick a dude's brains out then want me to suck your cock? What's wrong with me? What the fuck is wrong with *you*?" Marc glanced back at the doorway, back at the vagrant. Maybe it was a trick of the light, but the darkness now seemed empty. No bum. No dog. No sound they might have made.

Ash pinched the bridge of his nose, still waving the knife in his other hand.

"Ash?" Marc's voice was more timid than he would have liked. "Are you... Shit. Shit, that's it, isn't it? You're fucked up. You are *fucked up*!" It would have explained a lot. Ash didn't answer. He sniffed and opened his eyes, looking like he was trying to focus. "*Ash?*"

"Yeah!" he snarled. "Maybe, a bit. I needed something. I'm in fucking pain here, bitch."

Great. That was all he needed. Ash junked out of his mind with a bleeding cock, on the run from a man they'd murdered. Fucking great.

"I'm sorry," Marc said quietly.

Ash's stare was blank. "You're right," he said, finally snapping closed the knife and putting it back in his pocket. "You're right now, and you were right back there. That Dutch dude? That was not worthy. Shouldn't have done that. Not worthy at all. But you're worthy, aren't you, Marky? Most worthy guy I know. That's why I need you. Why I listen to you."

"What the fuck are you talking about? And since when have you ever listened to me?" Marc looked around once more at the grimy walls and the pothole off to his right. At the darkened, empty doorway. Where had the old guy gone?

"Did you have to bite my fucking dick?" Ash snarled.

"Did you have to make me suck you off? Right there? After you, what? Kicked a guy to death?"

Marc jumped, certain he was about to cop another fist in his face as Ash rounded on him. Instead, Ash gave him a nasty laugh, tightened by whatever junk had him soaring. Maybe he'd been high all night. It wouldn't have been the first time. Maybe that's what had made him so crazy, so stupid and horny.

"You want to kiss it better?" Ash taunted, thrusting out his crotch in a graceless movement.

"Fuck, no!"

Ash staggered toward him, thumbs hooked into the lip of his jeans. "Come on, Marky. I said I was sorry."

"No, actually you didn't."

Ash frowned at him for a moment. "You're right. Right again, Marky. Good for you."

Marc wanted to turn and run as Ash launched at him like a corpse walking. But his limbs refused to move. He chanced another look back at the doorway. The next thing he felt was Ash's hands around his shoulders, the guy's weight almost knocking him over.

Marc closed his eyes. Even now, having Ash's hands on him set his pulse racing. He hated it, just as he hated the strong, beautiful veins that raised a road map of well-worked muscle on Ash's arms. He hated knowing that under that flimsy, white tank was a body that set his cock twitching every time it drew near. And more than anything, he hated how sexy and goddamned sincere Ash's smile seemed in shadows that obscured any drugged-out imperfections from view. He quivered in Ash's grip, his stomach stirring. He hated the feeling of his dick twitching inside his jock. He only wished he could transfer that hate to Ash, whose lips now brushed his with easy tenderness. Whose eyes seemed so set on breaking his resolve, and whose forehead now rested gently against his own. Whose hands had slipped into the back side of his jeans.

Marc couldn't stand any more. He sighed as Ash took his hands out just long enough to pull the tank top up over his head and hold Marc tight against his shirtless body.

This time, Marc's gasp was so loud, he thought he'd cry out. If Ash was still in pain, he didn't show it, particularly not as he lifted Marc's shirt, hooked his fingers into Marc's jeans again and brushed a finger over Marc's cock.

"This is what you want from me, isn't it, Marky? This is why you stay."

There was no love in Ash's smile, but it didn't matter. There was desire. Maybe not for Marc. More likely, it was for the power Ash held over him, but Marc didn't care. He didn't care about who Ash was or what they'd done together. All that had scared him had given way to how Ash looked, smelt, and felt against his skin. It felt surreal, like Ash could genuinely be his. His own beautiful monster and murderer.

"No," Marc murmured.

"Shhhh..." Ash hushed against his lips. "I'm sorry, Marc. For real, I am."

Marc swallowed, unable to ignore how good those hands felt, stroking his nipples, tracing their line up to his underarms, over his collarbone and up the side of his neck, wrapping around it.

"Ash...? Ash!"

"Don't pretend like I'm not fond of you, Marky," Ash hissed as his grip tightened around Marc's throat. "I'm gonna make this a lot quicker than the last faggot I wasted. Close your eyes again and you'll barely feel it. Or scream, if you're that kind of pussy. Cool thing about this neighborhood, Marc? You can scream all you want. Nobody's coming."

Marc's brain was too starved of oxygen to be sure. He batted clumsily at Ash's body as Ash squeezed his windpipe, but it was too late. He hadn't even noticed Ash choke the strength from him. He'd been too focused on Ash's eyes, his lying smile, his hard body. All the tricks the bastard used on the johns, and Marc had fallen hard for them. He hated the erection that was too stupid and reflexive to realize the guy who'd given it life was killing him. He hated how his lust had blinded him. He hated that he was a fag.

Bark! Bark! Bark!

They'd been so close at first. Hell, they'd even turned a few tricks together. Put on a few two-man shows for the pervs who liked to watch. Ash had known these encounters had turned Marc on for real. Had it repulsed him all along? Had he been waiting for this moment? Had the thought entered his diseased brain that first time he'd pushed Marc away from the blowjob that had aroused him moments before? Had Marc just chosen to ignore that warning? And every warning since?

"I'm sorry, Marky." Nastiness filled Ash's every word. "Sorry I trusted you. Sorry I liked you. You've got nothing to offer me, faggot. Me or anyone else."

As the strength left his arms, Marc realized Ash hadn't heard the dog's barking. He hadn't reacted to it at all.

"Please Ash?" Marc choked. "Don't—"

"You're turning a pretty color there, Marky."

The stain of his sin. You remember?

What sin? What sin? What—

Ash released Marc with a start as a loud cry erupted from the darkness, followed by the crash and tinkling of a broken bottle.

"Oh lord!" wailed the drunk bum, staggering out into the light, waving the broken bottle neck in his stubby brown fist. "Let him be restored anewwww."

Marc clutched his bruised neck as his breath returned, the burning in his throat dulling to a faint ache. He lifted his head as he heard Ash cry out with a start.

"Hey watch it, nigger!" Ash barked, ducking the clumsy swoop of the man's bottle.

"Restored anewwww," the bum wailed again, lurching toward Ash before backing away with a broad smile, which seemed far too full of healthy teeth for Marc's liking. "Beg pardon, boys. Help an old man ou—"

Ash cut the bum's words short, shoving him hard in Marc's direction with a snarl.

Marc staggered, pulling himself narrowly out of the broken bottle's path. The bum rounded on them again, brandishing the bottle. He couldn't deal with this. Ash, he could handle. But this old guy getting up in their faces?

"Hey, last warning," said Ash, now standing at Marc's side. "Fuck off, man."

"You heard him," Marc agreed. He meant it, for the old guy's sake as much as his own.

"Awww. Hell, boys! Just a couple-a doll—"

"He said fuck off!" Marc shot his hand out, landing hard against the bum's grime-crusted jacket and sending him staggering back into the darkness. The man half spun on his heel and fell on his face with a sickening crunch. Marc couldn't see the bottle neck anywhere.

The two of them watched, mesmerized as thin trails of black smoke spread from beneath the man's body, covering the ground. It spread into a thick blanket, covering their ankles with a cold chill. Not just the damp cold of fog, but a bitter, biting cold. It hooked into Marc's skin like frozen fingers and wouldn't yield. The smoke spread into every dark nook and doorway.

"What'd you do?" Ash muttered. "What did you do, freak?"

"Nothing!"

It was a lie. He'd killed a man in anger, fueled by his own rage. This time, he couldn't hide behind Ash's killing blow.

Maybe he *was* a freak. Maybe Ash had a right to fear him. Maybe the two of them belonged together. Fucked up. Dangerous. Dead men walking.

No! An accident. The guy had been drunk. A horrible accident. That was all. Who the fuck was going to miss some bum anyway?

Smoke billowed from the doorway in which he'd first seen the man, breaking over their legs like shallow waves. A shape rose from it, sending wafts of smoke from the doorway as it rolled into its lumpen form, a crumpled, fetal shape with its arms curled up over its head. It trembled as Marc stepped closer, the icy smoke parting for him as it broke over his feet. Something about the size and trembling form of the shape seemed all too familiar. It was crying. The broken, twisted thing was whimpering. A man was inside that smoke.

"What is it?" Ash asked, fear bleeding through his cold tone.

Marc swallowed as he reached a hand into the freezing black mist, connecting with something smooth and cool. Something alive. Through the smoke, he finally made out the man's features. A young man, his nose long and dark. Below it, full, quivering lips. Sweat covered the rich, brown skin of the forehead, and the eyes were the color of thick, strong coffee. The image was as lovely a man as Marc had ever seen. And as it reached out, taking gentle hold of his fingers, he realized he'd seen it, many, many times before.

"Marc?" Ash called, all trace of a threat now gone as he barely whispered the name.

"Marc? Marc..." the image echoed.

Marc shuddered with a violence that scared him. He knew the strange man's touch. The way he'd touched his hand that first time in the bar. The way the man had stroked the back of his neck, too nervous to kiss him goodnight outside his parents' home. They'd more than made up for it on their next date, wrapping around each other and making out for hours at the Pub. He remembered the way the hand had held him so gently while they lazed under the brutal August sun in City Park, when they'd been too hot to move. That hand that had drunkenly groped his ass and teased his cock in the darkness, while a bunch of guys squinted to see the action. The last night he'd seen this stranger, whose body had been found four days later, crumpled, beaten and broken.

Shreveport.

"Marc? What is it? Shit, what's...?" Ash's words fell away as he saw the familiar face. And the strange apparition saw him, its face stretching and contorting as it pointed to Ash in a silent scream.

"No!" Marc howled as the thing's dark jaw tore away, its face crumbling into nothing, its beautiful skin stretched and shriveled into black, crinkling ash. Marc turned away, only to see the grinning face of Ghede Nibo, the loa fairy. The psychopomp and keeper of the dead who had aided him, fueling his courage and anger.

Now, he remembered it all. Love for love. Blood for blood.

He ripped the knife from his pocket and in one swift movement, thrust it deep up into Ash's gut. Again, and again he pushed it between Ash's ribs, ignoring the terror that had filled his blue eyes. The eyes of the monster who'd stolen Antoine from him. Who'd stalked and destroyed his lover like a predator, high on drugs and hatred. The one he'd finally found but not recognized. The one whose trust he'd slowly earned.

His prey, whose blood now dripped from his knife and hand.

The loa had kept its word, protecting his memory and soul. Taken from him the man he was, just to be absolutely sure Ash wouldn't see through his lie. And Ash hadn't. Even when the spirit had denied him all memory of Antoine, all memory of Ash's crime. The spirit had seen his plan through to the last exquisite detail.

Still soaked with Ash's blood, he fell to his knees. Exhausted. Vindicated.

He watched Ash's dark, crumpled form try to roll over, ignoring its faint groans and whimpers as a narrow river of blood seeped from the bastard's body. It seemed like so little. How many times had he stabbed him? Five? Seven? The pallid color of a white forearm emerged from the darkness, slick with blood. With one loud groan, a pale face stained with tears, blood, and grime followed. He forced himself up onto his side, fixing his steely blue gaze on Marc and refusing to budge.

"M…Marc," the man mewled, his voice almost silent, buried under the rain. "Marky?"

For a moment, they could only sit, staring at each other. He could feel the knife bouncing in his twitching fingers, warm with Ash's blood.

"Marc?"

Marc bellowed as rage propelled him atop his prey again, straddling the bleeding, mutilated body, forcing it back down onto the ground as he brought the knife down over and over. Each thrust plunged deeper into the man's neck. He cupped his hand over the bastard's mouth to muffle his screams, which diminished until the monster could barely manage a gurgling whine. He grimaced as he severed an artery, sending a spray of blood across his own face. It didn't matter. There would be no healing. No surprises. No redemption or second chances for the bastard murderer.

When he could no longer feel the man's breath under his fingers, he ripped the blade across what remained of the throat for good measure. But the neck was now so ragged, his blade snagged on a bone that almost yanked it out of his hand. The bastard's blue eyes stared up at him. Wide, open, imploring his mercy. He'd seen those beautiful eyes before. With every apology for every slight. The mask. The act. The eyes that had seduced him.

He brought his fist down once, twice…until a trickle of blood ran from the shattered temple, over what had been Ash's face, which stared aimlessly into the darkness, shunted into an alien, upward angle impossible for anyone still alive.

He threw the knife into the darkness and backed away from the broken corpse. He could no longer see its grim eyes, only the shadow of the open throat he'd destroyed. He averted his gaze, which landed on the crumpled form of the hobo, felled by his own bottle.

The man's toenails were pink.

He squinted, casting what he was seeing into marked doubt. He hadn't seen it before, but now, caught in the dim back entrance light of the warehouse, there was nothing natural about that color. The poor bastard had met his end on the edge of a broken liquor bottle, feet naked all except for ten perfectly buffed, vivid pink toes.

Fucking crazy bastard. A bastard he'd killed by… accident? Like Ash's 'accident' with the Dutch guy? Fuck!

He hadn't noticed the fog return until the cold damp had shrouded his hands. The pavement felt like ice, even in the warm summer rain and crushing humidity. The fog washed over his lap and crossed his belly with a faint sigh that felt so strange, he barely noticed it envelop the bodies of the hobo and the murderer.

He shivered as it rose higher, steadily increasing in density as it crept up his arms and chest, until he could no longer see a damn thing, not even a hand held up inches from his face. The black fog grew denser still, starting to tickle against his skin. Then itch. It felt like… Damn it! It felt as if he'd been covered with goddamn cockroaches, all running up and down his skin, laying tiny eggs in his pores and hatching them just as fast. Each effort he made to scratch himself met only the sensation of plunging his fingers into the crawling mass, unable to get a grip on his own flesh. Then, it began to burn, and he began to scream, and scream, and scream, knowing nobody could hear.

He couldn't even hear himself.

KYLE

Kyle tried to open his eyes, but even the dim glow of the nearest streetlight stung them. Instead he lay there, letting the cold, soothing rain drops bounce off his face and body until he was at last able to move. His head felt like it had been filled up with rocks. His legs weren't faring much better, protesting every inch of movement as he dragged one over the other and tried to right himself on his knees. When at last he succeeded, ignoring the sting of wet gravel that dug into them, staying up on all fours took all his energy.

The taste in his mouth was a rancid mix of blood, semen, vomit, and cigarettes. He coughed violently to clear his throat, grateful for the rush of fresh, if humid, air that filled his lungs. As the turning in his stomach slowed and his breathing regained its steady rhythm, he felt the cold drops bouncing off his exposed back and butt. He arched them into the air before bending back, turning his face to the sky and sticking out his tongue. He couldn't remember water ever tasting so good. He wished the rain were heavier. That it'd pour down in one almighty torrent that... Fuck that. Kyle wanted a bath. Badly.

Kyle.

His name was Kyle.

"Kyle," he murmured under his breath. "Kyle. Kyle. My name is Kyle. Kyle. My name is…"

He rolled over, pressing the wet gravel into his back. A stupid grin crossed his face as he silently mouthed the words over and over. It was done. Oh, god! What had it been? Almost a year? It didn't matter. He was himself again.

He finally opened his eyes, letting the gentle rain splash his eyelids and lashes. The light, the street signs, the trees, the buildings, even the yellow moon blurred almost beyond recognition. Fuck. What had he just been through? He carefully rolled onto his side, trying to focus on the dark shape a few feet away. He could just make out its slim shoulders, long, powerful legs, and the darkness of a full head of short, tightly curled black hair.

His grin spread wider still, until he broke into a quiet laugh.

The figure didn't move. Little by little, Kyle edged his way toward it until he closed his hand over its shoulder. Antoine. He'd known it. He'd fucking known it was him, instantly recognizing the warmth, texture, and smell of his skin and hair. Kyle grinned as his hands rediscovered every familiar bump and ripple of Antoine's body. When he wrapped his arm around his lover's chest, he could no longer contain his tears. Warm drops of joy and relief ran down his face, mingling with the rain on the skin of the man that bastard had stolen. And where was that bastard now? Keeping company with the dead and damned? Kyle had no way, nor any desire to know.

Unable to resist, he kissed Antoine's shoulders and the back of his neck over and over and over, pressing his cheek to the man's skin, unwilling to risk the brutality of a cruel joke. It was all real, down to the steady beat of his lover's heart beneath the palm of Kyle's hand as he pulled him closer. Realizing they were both naked, he tried to warm Antoine's legs with what meager body heat he had to share. Were their clothes somewhere nearby? It didn't matter. They'd be warm soon enough. Home, warm, safe, and most of all, together.

"Thank you," he murmured in between kisses, unsure of what to call the spirit, or even if it could hear. "Thank you, thank you, thank you."

Antoine stirred in his arms, releasing a faint and all too familiar sigh, followed by a petulant whine that in that moment was the sweetest sound Kyle had ever heard.

"Shhh," he said, squeezing gently. "It's okay. Everything's going to be okay."

He had expected more pain. More fear. Screaming. Crying. A horrible distortion or perversion of his lover's form. But it was all his Antoine., exactly as he remembered, sleeping peacefully in the cold rain as if the street were his very own bed.

Their own bed. Kyle grinned again, brushing the back of Antoine's neck with his lips.

"Stop it," the man whispered, shifting his shoulders.

As Antoine's eyes flew open, he knitted his dark eyebrows and pushed out of Kyle's grasp.

"It's okay. There's…" Kyle trailed off, not knowing where to begin his explanation.

Antoine eased himself up, face turned away from Kyle as he straightened his back. He flinched, shielding his eyes from the stinging streetlight.

Kyle watched the steady rise and fall of his lover's back as the simple act of breathing returned. He dived forward as Antoine coughed violently, putting a steady hand on his back. "It's all right. It's all right. Take it slow." He could see Antoine's lips moving, but the sound refused to come. Questions silenced by their own ridiculousness. In time. They had to give it time.

He remembered it all. What if Antoine didn't? What if he remembered only some of what had happened or had forgotten Kyle entirely? Worse, what if he remembered everything?

"We need to get you inside," he said, rubbing his hand over Antoine's shoulder.

With a swallow that seemed to pain him, Antoine agreed with a determined nod. Memory or no memory, Kyle couldn't expect Antoine to feel himself again in the pouring rain, now so heavy, he could barely make out the man's quiet sobs.

"Hey," he said, wrapping his arms around the man's chest. "I've got you. I'm never letting you go again. You hear me? Not ever."

Cold fingers closed around his wrist, falling perfectly still. Then, Antoine began to shake.

"Hey," Kyle said. "Hey, what's wrong? Anto—"

Antoine caught his jaw with the back of a closed fist before he could finish. Kyle bit back a scream as Antoine twisted the wrist he'd taken hold of and pushed it back so far he thought it might break, only letting him go with a hard shove that sent him sprawling to the ground.

Kyle swore as the loose gravel grazed his knees and hands. He'd pushed him. Antoine had thrown him off into the dirt like garbage. He watched, eyes wide as his lover staggered to his feet, tottering as he managed to right himself, before turning his fury on Kyle once more.

"What...what the...?" Kyle stammered. "Hey, it's me! It's just—"

Antoine was on him in an instant, teeth bared, fingers like talons, reaching for his neck as Kyle tried to throw him off. Unable to reach his target, Antoine instead settled for using his fists. Over and over, Kyle felt the punches find their mark on his cheek. But it was the words that hurt more.

"Stay away from me! Come near me again and I'll beat the shit out of you, you evil cunt!"

The words caught in Kyle's throat, but what was there to say? This wasn't his Antoine. It couldn't be. Not like this. Not with so much rage and hate. Something had gone wrong. Something had changed.

"P...pl...please?" he murmured through a mess of blood. He tried mouthing Antoine's name, but nothing would come. The man just stared back at him, his dark eyes colder than the rain. Colder than anything he'd ever felt as they pierced him.

"Motherfucker..." The man hissed, rising to his full height. "Motherfucker!"

Kyle winced, arms flying up to protect his head as Antoine sent one final kick into his side. It wasn't strong, but it might as well have sent him flying across the lake for the impact he felt. "Please?" he sobbed, almost silent in the rain. "Don't leave me."

"Where are my clothes? Fuck you, *where are they*, asshole?" Antoine screamed at him. "You're fucking pathetic." With a few steps into the shadows, he was gone.

Kyle lay sobbing and weeping silently into the street, ignoring the pain that consumed his face, his gut, and most of all, his heart. Slowly, he forced himself to move, staggering to his feet and out onto the open street. A car's headlights blinded him as it trundled past.

"Hey, the strip joint's that way, dumb ass!" jeered the driver.

There had to be someone he could stop. Someone he could beg for help, who could take him to a hospital. Hell, even the cops might be better at this point. The glow of Frenchman Street lay not two blocks ahead, and there seemed to be more streetlights now. He held up a hand to shield his eyes once more.

That wasn't right. He stared the tattoo that ended on his wrist, then glanced down the length of his body before turning to catch a look at himself in the window of a parked car.

He shook his head, backing away slowly, unable to take his eyes off the reflection until he turned and ran. He didn't stop until he was back where it had happened, an empty lot behind a warehouse like dozens of others all over the Bywater.

Once hidden in the dark, he put his head in his hands and screamed.

KYLE

Each morning he'd felt unable to tell when exactly his eyes had opened. When they'd at last caught up to the slow return of consciousness. Unable to remember when or how his dreams had surrendered to reality. The mattress seemed just as big as it had the first night he'd woken alone. The first night, then the second. He could no longer remember a night he'd slept soundly.

He swallowed, trying to dismiss the erection that taunted him beneath the sheet. Nothing seemed less appealing than sex just now. He barely noticed the smell of thin sheets that reeked with his sweat, nor could he tell where his own scent ended and the dead man's began. All the nights they'd spent together. Nights of sex, fear, anger, and some strange state he could hardly call love. But it had been something, and meant something to the man he'd been. And like the smell of their bodies on his sheets, its meaning remained, clinging so tightly to him he could no longer make out the join between himself and the all too real and visceral illusion he'd lived for he didn't know how long.

The thing had relieved him so cleanly of his memories the first time. Why not now? Wasn't he owed at least that kindness for the risk he'd taken? For all he'd lost?

Now, as he rolled in his own dried sweat, he understood he was owed nothing.

He staggered wearily to his feet, kicking the sheets away and trying to catch a breeze across his naked chest. The air was still and thick, as it had been all summer, tainted by the faint, putrid smell of rot and sick. He crossed the room and nudged open the shutters, staring down at the Quarter street slowly stirring to life, catching a fresh whiff of that aroma so particular to Bourbon Street before noon on a weekend.

He lazily scooped up his phone, checking the message that flashed on and off.

Back on the bar tonight or you're done. Last chance.

He groaned, tossing the phone back down on the table and leaning against the shutters with a loud clatter, trying to block the smell of the street beneath him and the sounds of the couple arguing in the apartment next door. She'd yell first, then he'd scream back. It had been the same every morning, every weekend.

Fuck. Why was there no breeze in here? He winced as the foul morning air of Bourbon Street found his nose, though he knew he couldn't have smelled much better. The cool tiles in the bathroom were almost a relief as he turned on the shower, hard and cold as it would go. It wasn't near cold enough. He let the tepid water pummel him clean for five, maybe ten minutes, leaning back and letting it hit his face. That face. Maybe if he let the water run long enough, it would tear away. He rested his head against the shower tiles, his tears, long exhausted. His cock shriveled under the cool water. Again, he ignored it, turning off the faucet and letting the water drip from his body as the thick air merged with it, congealing on his flesh.

Feeling nowhere near clean, he mopped away what moisture he could, tossed the towel to the wooden floor and stared at his phone once more.

His phone? He felt the urge to laugh, cut short by a glimpse of his bathroom mirror. At the face that stared back at him, once handsome and beguiling, now drawn out and pale, like it had been trembling and weeping for days. Of course, he had.

He didn't look away. Not this time. This time he approached the mirror, let the cracks, pocks and blemishes widen in his sight, his hollow cheeks deepen as he approached his reflection. He swallowed, an ugly lump forcing its way down his throat, into the pit of his stomach. He gently touched the death's head that grinned below his navel. Then looked down at the snake that coiled around his arm, its vicious fangs buried deep in his wrist.... *lest you become the very monster you seek.*

The loa's words haunted his memory, mocking him with their unmistakable clarity. He shivered as he and the reflection made eye contact, just for an instant. Those eyes, he could not stand. Those frozen orbs that had looked on him with...disdain? Cruelty? Lust? Maybe even affection? The last eyes Antoine had seen before he'd died.

He refused to dramatize it. Those eyes were his now. There was no avoiding them. Nor the tattoos, nor the body, nor the dirty, sandy blonde hair that crowned the awful visage. All his own now.

He rested his hands against the sink, steadying himself against the tearing sensation that wracked his stomach, until eventually, he forced himself to look into the eyes once more. Cold. Blue.

"It's just skin," he murmured, finally loosening his grip on the sink, releasing the tension that had gripped his toes and letting them settle on the tiles. "It's just skin. It's just skin. It's just skin. It's just skin. It's just skin. It's just skin..."

Also by Christian Baines:

PUPPET BOY

A school in turmoil over its senior play, a sly career as a
teenage gigolo, an unpredictable girlfriend with damage of her
own, and a dangerous housebreaker tied up downstairs. Any
of these would make a great plot for budding filmmaker
Eric's first movie. Unfortunately, they're his real life. When
Julien, a handsome wannabe actor, transfers to Eric's class,
he's a distraction, a rival, and one complication too many. Yet

Eric can't stop thinking about him. Helped by Eric's
girlfriend, Mary, they embark on a project that dangerously
crosses the line between filmmaking and reality. As the boys
become close, Eric soon wants to cross other lines entirely.
Does Julien feel the same way, or is Eric being used on the
gleefully twisted path to fame?

THE BEAST WITHOUT

Reylan is everything a Sydney vampire aspires to be: wealthy, handsome and independent, carefully feeding off companions plucked from the gay bars of Oxford Street.

When one of those companions is killed by Jorgas, a hot-headed young werewolf prowling his streets, Reylan reluctantly puts his cherished lifestyle of blood and boys on hold to help a mysterious alliance of supernatural beings track down the beast. It can't be that hard...not when Jorgas keeps coming after him.

But there's more to this werewolf than a body count and a bad attitude. As their relationship grows deeper and more twisted, Reylan tastes Jorgas's blood, reawakening desires the vampire had thought long dead. And what evolves between them may be far more dangerous than some rival predator in the dark...

THE ORCHARD OF FLESH

Reylan's last assignment for The Arcadia Trust brought a
rebellious human servant under his roof, and a volatile
werewolf lover named Jorgas into his bed, leaving the self-
reliant Blood Shade—known to the outside world as
vampires—in no hurry to risk his immortality for them again.

But when a new terror starts disappearing humans from a
bad part of town, Reylan must do everything in his power to
keep Sydney's supernatural factions from the brink of war.
Having an ambitious, meddlesome human in the mix is only
going to make things worse...especially when that human is
Jorgas's father.

Reylan will need all his determination and cunning to keep
the peace under his roof, between the night's power brokers,
and in his lover's troubled heart.

SINS OF THE SON

Abandoned by his werewolf lover, the only thing Reylan wants is to return to his vampire life of blood and beautiful boys. It's a solid plan, until his first meal as a single man tries to kill him.

Hoping to free his young would-be assassin from the religious zealots that sent him, Reylan enlists the help of Iain Grieg, a charismatic priest with unsettling knowledge of the night's secrets.

Surrounded by conflicting agendas and an army fuelled by hate, Reylan fights to secure his future, if he can only trust the mysterious priest and bury the ghosts of the past.

CPSIA information can be obtained
at www.ICGtesting.com
Printed in the USA
BVHW041658230620
581833BV00003B/13